"But he did promise to return. So maybe you can do better next time."

"Better?" Charlotte gave her sister a wry grin. "Are you insinuating I did a poor job with this conversation?"

Anastasia took a step back and held up her hands. "No, not at all. You were likely your usual self, keeping all talk to the bookshop, books, and reading."

"And what else is there to discuss when a customer comes in to shop?"

"Well, you could share a little about yourself."

"With someone I've just met? I wouldn't be so presumptuous."

Her sister sighed and rolled her eyes. "You're hopeless."

"No," Charlotte countered. "Merely practical." She had such fun baiting her sister and playing to her conniving, matchmaking schemes. But the last thing she needed was a young girl interfering with her customers.

"And that will never secure you a man," her sister said under her breath.

"What was that?"

Anastasia jerked up her head. "I said, uh, as the owner, I can understand."

AMBER STOCKTON is a freelance Web designer and author whose articles and short stories have appeared in local, national, and international publications. Her writing career began as a columnist for her high school and college newspapers. Her first publication in a book appeared in the form of nine contributions (as a single!) to *101 Ways to Romance Your Marriage* by Debra White Smith. She is a member of American Christian Fiction Writers and Historical Romance Writers. Some of her hobbies include traveling, music, photography, and MOPS. At age three, she learned to read and hasn't put down books since. She lives with her husband and fellow author, Stuart Vaughn Stockton, and their two children in colorful Colorado. Visit her website to learn more or to contact her: www.amberstockton.com.

Books by Amber Miller
HP784—Promises, Promises
HP803—Quills & Promises
HP823—Deceptive Promises

Books by Amber Stockton
HP843—Copper and Candles
HP867—Hearts and Harvest
HP867—Patterns and Progress

Bound by Grace

Amber Stockton

Heartsong Presents

I want to thank JoAnne Simmons for the golden opportunity to write for this club and for helping me get my foot in the door. I also want to thank my copyeditors, Rachel Overton and Becky Fish. My writing has only improved because of you. Finally, this book is dedicated to my readers, who have faithfully continued to purchase and read my books. I wouldn't be an author without you!

A note from the Author:
I love to hear from my readers! You may correspond with me by writing:

Amber Stockton
Author Relations
PO Box 721
Uhrichsville, OH 44683

ISBN 978-1-61626-580-9

BOUND BY GRACE

one

Brandywine, Delaware, 1881

"So, was your venture successful? Did the gentleman have what he promised? Were you able to locate it?"

Charlotte Pringle's youngest sister barely allowed her to step through the door to the bookshop before the verbal interrogation began. Her assistant, Laura, looked up from behind the front counter, the same place Charlotte had left her nearly two hours ago.

Charlotte pushed back and untied the hood on her cape. After inhaling the familiar smells of leather, wood, and vanilla incense, she gave Anastasia a teasing grin. "Might I have a moment to relax from my journey before you plague me with questions? I might need to burn some lavender incense if you continue in this fashion."

Anastasia looked as if she might bust a seam in her daffodil walking dress, but she could wait a few more moments.

"Laura." Charlotte addressed her assistant. "Thank you for tending the store in my absence."

"It was my pleasure, Miss Charlotte." Laura averted her gaze and wrung her hands on the apron she wore. "If you have no other need for me at the front, I'll return to reconciling our inventory."

"That will be fine, Laura. Thank you again."

Just one year younger than Charlotte's own age of twenty, Laura wasn't much for conversation. But she worked hard and was quite thorough. Given Anastasia's fanciful notions, Charlotte appreciated having someone dependable to help her.

"So—o. . ." Anastasia splayed her hands on the edge of one of the front tables, barely acknowledging Laura's departure. "What was the result?"

With a calm that contradicted the butterflies fluttering in her stomach, Charlotte reached into her satchel and withdrew a worn but well-kept volume of *Robinson Crusoe*. She closed her eyes and ran her fingers across the smooth surface of the binding, her mind replaying the name written just inside the front cover. A first edition. Once owned by her great-grandmother's great-grandmother, Raelene Strattford. Charlotte's mother loved telling the story of how the book played into the courting of Gustaf and Raelene. But somewhere along the line, the book had been lost. A chance meeting with a bookstore owner in Philadelphia alerted Charlotte to the book's location. After six generations of history, she had finally brought it back into the family once more.

"You did find it!" Anastasia clasped her hands together just beneath her chin, her bright eyes resembling those of a child who'd just stepped into an ice-cream shop. Leave it to her sister to be overly dramatic.

Charlotte shook her head. "Yes, although judging by your reaction, one might think *you* were the one who had been searching for three years to find this treasure."

"Can a girl not be truly happy for her sister?" The gleam in Anastasia's eyes matched Charlotte's excitement. "I love books as much as you do." An impish grin overtook her lips as she turned away and moved from behind the counter, assuming an air of nonchalance. "Besides, one day some of these cherished tomes may very well become mine. And I have already been making a list."

Charlotte raised one eyebrow. "Oh, you have, have you?" She crossed her arms. "Suppose I decide to live far longer than you. What will you do then?"

"Borrow them when you are not looking," her sister said with a shrug.

Anastasia winked and pranced away toward the four long aisles of books, but not before Charlotte reached out and tugged one of the bouncing locks hanging down her back. How nice it must be. So carefree and young. Of course, Anastasia was almost fourteen. And she'd already had at least two young men express interest in pursuing a courtship with her. Not so young, after all.

If only those young men had older brothers or knew of some men who weren't already engaged or married. The selection seemed to grow thinner with each passing day. Charlotte sometimes wondered if she'd ever meet a man who understood her passion. Her friends told her she needed to give up the bookshop if she hoped to find a suitable match, but that was out of the question. She loved her books too much. And if a man couldn't love her along with everything she brought to the relationship, she'd rather remain alone.

As the eldest daughter, however, she owed it to her parents to make a suitable match. With her older brother married and poised to follow in their father's footsteps in gunpowder manufacturing, working closely with the du Pont family, the mantle now rested on her shoulders. If another season passed without any prospects, her parents might be forced to choose someone for her. She prayed that wouldn't be the case, but she'd honor them if it happened.

"Charlotte?" Anastasia called from the back of the shop. "Where did you shelve that copy of *Emma* you had last week? I can't seem to find it. Someone didn't borrow it, did they?" She gasped. "Or purchase it? I have wanted to read it for several days, but I had to finish *Pride and Prejudice* first. I shall simply swoon if it's gone."

Charlotte erupted into laughter. "It's the next aisle over, you silly goose, with the rest of the books by Jane Austen."

She peeked down the aisle and caught her sister's eye. "As much time as you spend here, you would think you'd know the location of every book by heart."

"No, that honor belongs only to you, dear sister." Anastasia grinned as she flounced around the corner to the appropriate shelf.

Charlotte smiled. Yes, she did know each and every precious volume and the treasured locations where they rested. She reached out and caressed the spine of the nearest title. Some days, the books served as better companions than her friends or the latest unsuitable suitor her parents attempted to send her way.

"Found it!" Her sister's voice floated to the front of the shop, preceding Anastasia's appearance by mere seconds. She clutched the book to her chest. "I'll have it back to you in less than a week. No one will know it's gone." She pursed her lips. "Except you, of course."

Charlotte reached out and tipped her sister's chin with her finger. "Just be certain you don't allow any more matchmaking ideas to enter that pretty little head of yours. Remember what happened the last time you attempted to orchestrate a rendezvous between Jeremiah Graham and Amanda Stewart?"

"Oh, must you remind me of that again?" Anastasia held up the book to hide her face. "You have to admit they did appear rather fond of each other." She peered over the top of the book. "How was I to know their grandmothers were sisters?"

"You would have had you been paying more attention to the conversations around you and less to your latest matchmaking schemes." Charlotte rolled her eyes. "Honestly, I can't fathom why you continue to interfere in other people's lives in such a manner. Why not allow young ladies and gentlemen to choose for themselves who they shall marry?

The results are so much better that way."

"Not always." Anastasia wagged one finger. "Do you recall how I arranged for shy and unassuming Paulina Whetstone to accidentally bump into the much-sought-after Matthew Adams? Those two likely would never have given each other a moment's notice had I not moved things along a bit." She took on an air of smug triumph. "Even you cannot deny how perfectly suited they are for each other."

"It is true." Charlotte pressed a finger to her lips. "I have never seen either one of them so happy, nor more suitably matched." She shook a warning finger in her sister's direction. "But that is not the case with most of your attempts. And I fear reading that book"—she gestured toward the volume her sister held—"will only make matters worse."

"Or it might improve my skills," Anastasia countered. "Perhaps I only need a lesson or two in observation skills. If I paid closer attention, I might become far more successful than I have been."

"And if you do not, I shall be forced to go behind you to clean up the pieces of your failed attempts." Charlotte covered her sister's hands with her own, imploring her with her eyes. "Just promise to be more careful next time. Please?"

Anastasia tilted her head, peering up at Charlotte. "Very well," she sighed. "But I suppose I should tell you I have already selected the fortunate young lady who will become the next focus of my attentions."

Charlotte raised both eyebrows. "Oh? And who might that be?"

Her sister stepped out of reach and fairly skipped the few steps toward the back door of the shop. She placed one hand on the doorknob and pulled open the door leading to the common courtyard area behind the buildings. Peering over her shoulder, she tossed her sister an impish grin. "You." With that, she was gone.

The final word hung in the air like an ominous storm cloud about to release everything it held. Charlotte turned her face heavenward and sent up a silent prayer asking when the cloud finally did burst, she wouldn't get too wet.

&

More than a week later, Charlotte marveled over how many new customers had visited her shop. It seemed as if someone had posted banners around the area, announcing the shop's location. But she wasn't about to complain. She *did* own the only shop that both sold and loaned books between here and Philadelphia. The increased patronage helped both her sales and the shop's reputation. If each one of those who visited her shop told one or two other people, she might have to consider taking on another assistant and extending the hours she was open to the public.

Even the courier had been making more frequent visits. He seemed to deliver a letter every other day from someone inquiring about this title or that, asking if she had it in stock and if she might set it aside for them until they had the opportunity to come in person. One such letter had just been delivered yesterday, but Charlotte had read it at least a dozen times since. She kept it folded and tucked in her pocket. During a brief lull, she withdrew the now-worn paper again and read:

> *To the Owner of Cobblestone Books:*
> *I have recently learned of the existence of your shop from various acquaintances. It appears I might need to pay a visit, but I wanted to write and notify you of my possible arrival beforehand, for I did not wish to appear unannounced. Since the purpose of my visit is to locate a handful of specific titles, I would like to make you aware of those titles in the hopes you might secure them beforehand and have them ready. My niece is rather fond of reading,*

and she has read everything I've given her at least twice over. Enclosed is a complete list of titles I would like to locate. Any of them will suffice, as I do not expect you to have them all available. I shall be happy to compensate you for your time and assistance. Please use the address accompanying this letter for any reply. Thank you for your time. I look forward to visiting as soon as time permits.

With regards,
Richard Baxton

Charlotte couldn't place her finger on exactly what drew her to the letter, but something about the words the gentleman chose and the manner in which he framed them spoke to her. His obvious love for his niece might be part of the attraction, as well. After all, how could she turn away a doting uncle who wanted to appease his niece's insatiable appetite for reading? She felt a kinship with the girl already.

Not wanting to allow any more time to pass, Charlotte opened a drawer of her desk behind the counter and withdrew a sheet of paper. She reached for the pen and dipped it in ink, preparing to compose a reply.

Dear Mr. Baxton:
I have received your note and would be honored to welcome you to my shop. The books you listed are ones I already have among my inventory. So you need not allow any more time to pass before making arrangements to visit. I have set the titles aside as you requested. Please come at your earliest convenience. I look forward to meeting you.

Sincerely,
Miss Charlotte Pringle
Owner

That should do it. Charlotte read over her response three

times, making certain it didn't sound too forward but wanting it to be both sincere and professional. With a nod of satisfaction, she folded the page and tucked it inside an envelope, sealing it with wax and addressing the outside as Mr. Baxton had instructed. The next time the courier arrived, she would give him the letter to post. After that, she had only to wait for Mr. Baxton's arrival.

Oh, how she prayed it wouldn't be long.

❧

Richard Baxton stepped into the dark study, illuminated by the lone gas lamp on the desk. He'd been procrastinating for several weeks, but this task needed attention. Everything about the room seemed to bear a direct connection to his older brother. From the rich Aubusson rug covering most of the floor and the heavy velvet drapes at the windows to the custom-built, floor-to-ceiling shelves holding a wide selection of books, references, and ledgers, every nook and cranny said Elliott Baxton had once spent most of his time here.

Even the leather chair bore evidence of Elliott's presence. Richard pulled the chair away from the desk and sat down. He felt like a traitor, sitting there. This seat didn't belong to him. It belonged to his brother. What right did he have to sit in it now? Maybe he should take the work needing to be done and return to his own place. But that would mean taking his niece away from the only home she'd ever known. It had been only two months since the accident, and barely four weeks since she'd come home from the hospital. Richard didn't have the heart to pull her away.

He raised his head and gazed at the wall. Portraits of his family's patriarchs going back a half dozen generations lined the wall. They seemed to stare at him in condescension, their expectations high that he not be the one to see the family business fall to ruin. And he'd do everything in his power to see that it didn't. Even if working with his hands and managing the building of the ships suited him better than overseeing business affairs, he wouldn't disappoint his family.

With a sigh, Richard shifted his attention to the ledger on the desk in front of him. He'd happily pass on this task to someone else—anyone else—but at the moment, no one available possessed the necessary skills. Truth be told, he didn't either. But their accountant had left just before the accident, and Richard hadn't hired anyone else yet. As the new owner, he had to get it done.

Numbers had never been his strength. He'd left that to his more studious older brother. Now, with Elliott gone, the task fell to him. How he wished he'd paid more attention during his schooling. But if Richard allowed his thoughts to drift anymore, another week would pass and the ledgers still wouldn't be settled. The release of the funds associated with his brother's estate depended on the accounts being balanced. Like it or not, he had to get to work.

Three hours later, Richard drummed his fingers on top of the ledger, tempted to let his head fall to the desktop. He'd been over the numbers in every column at least a dozen times, and they simply refused to cooperate. How had the accounting gotten so out of hand in such a short time? Or was it him? Could his figuring be that rusty?

His brother had repeatedly told him how organized the financial side of the business was. Their former accountant possessed a degree from one of the finest schools in Philadelphia. So why could Richard not balance the spreadsheet? What was he doing wrong?

Steady footfalls sounded in the hallway outside the study. Eager for the interruption, Richard looked up as the butler appeared in the doorway. The man cleared his throat.

"Pardon the interruption, sir, but a missive has just arrived for you."

"Harrison, please tell me it isn't another note from our lawyer." Richard stood and rubbed his temples with his fingers. "I might be tempted to ask you to return it without my reading it."

"No, sir. This is not from the lawyer." The butler glanced down at the envelope. "It is from a Miss Charlotte Pringle, sir. Of Cobblestone Books." He started to turn away. "Shall I leave it on the tray in the front hall?"

Charlotte Pringle? From the bookstore Richard had contacted? He'd expected the owner to be a gentleman.

"No!" Richard stood and nearly toppled his leather chair. He spoke more calmly. "I will take it." He held out his hand.

Harrison stepped to the dark cherry desk and handed the letter to Richard. "Will that be all, sir?"

"Thank you, Harrison. Yes, that will be all. I will call upon you if a reply is necessary."

"Very good, sir."

Richard lowered himself into the well-worn chair once more and stared at the envelope. If this response was as he hoped, one of his less pressing dilemmas would be solved. He slit the seal and removed the single sheet of paper.

So, the owner was a lady. Or perhaps a matron. She might even be an old spinster with poor matrimonial prospects who had chosen to run an old bookshop instead. Glancing at the distinctive feminine script, Richard made up his mind. Definitely a lady. And judging by the feel of the paper as well as the words chosen, a lady of class. The carefully centered seal in the wax should have told him that from the start.

Richard read the letter three times, a pleased smile forming on his lips. The owner had signed the letter with a *Miss* preceding her name. That usually indicated a young lady, although it didn't rule out the spinster possibility. Nevertheless, he had a mission in mind, and Miss Pringle had not only obliged him with a response, but she had also set aside every title he'd requested. His niece would be thrilled.

"Are you busy?"

Richard started at the young voice. "Grace, what did I tell you about sneaking up on me like that?" It had been almost a month, yet sharing a home with a child still felt foreign.

Grace gave him an apologetic look mixed with a hint of indignation. "I didn't sneak up on you, Uncle Richard. I came down the hall as I normally do." She placed her hands on the large wheels to each side of her chair and moved them forward, bringing her into the study. Her expression reflected both sorrow and melancholy. "Besides, one cannot exactly be silent in a contraption like this."

"You have a point." Richard nodded, his heart going out to his niece, confined to a chair after the carriage accident that took her parents. "I suppose I was lost in thought. Do forgive me for snapping."

"Oh, I could never be cross with you, Uncle." Her eyes reflected sadness, yet a pixie-like smile graced her face. "Who else is going to get me every book I could ever want? As well as all the sugar sticks I can eat?"

An answering grin parted his lips. "Now who said anything about sugar sticks?"

She pressed her hands against the wheels and raised herself up. "You mean I truly can have any book I want?" Grace wheeled closer. "Does that mean you heard back from one of the shops?"

"As a matter of fact. . ." Richard stood and moved around the desk to stand in front of his niece. He kneeled to be at eye level with her, placing his hands over hers. "Yes, I did."

Eagerness filled her expression. "What did they say?"

Richard glanced back toward the desk then again at Grace. "The owner has each and every title on your list, and she has set them aside for us to come see."

Grace's eyes widened. "She?" A wrinkle formed in the middle of her brow, and she pressed her lips into a thin line. "That doesn't mean the owner is a dour old spinster, does it?"

"That will be enough of that, young lady," Richard reprimanded. "We have yet to meet Miss Pringle. I'll not have you forming assumptions and passing judgment before we meet her." Of course he had done that very thing moments before. He'd do well to heed his own instructions.

Appearing immediately contrite, Grace lowered her gaze. "Yes, sir. I'm sorry."

Richard tipped up her chin with the crook of his finger. "Very well. Shall we begin making plans for our journey?"

"Do you mean I can join you?" The shift from contrition to joy nearly caused Richard to fall back. Ah, the exuberance of youth.

"I would not have it any other way, my dear." He tapped Grace's nose and smiled, silently praying Cobblestone Books had street-level access.

two

"What do you think he looks like?" Anastasia held the feather duster in one hand, swiping at every visible surface in the bookshop. Charlotte's parents didn't force her to work, but Anastasia said she enjoyed helping. "Do you think he's an older, portly sort of gentleman? Or perhaps one of those men who do nothing but read books, wear spectacles, and hide away in their houses?" She paused and held the duster across her chest, a dreamy-eyed look entering her eyes. "Oh! Perhaps he's dashing and young and charming, and he'll come to sweep you off your feet!" Anastasia punctuated her remark by sweeping the duster across the floor.

Charlotte continued straightening the front counter and sighed. She needed to limit the number of romance stories her sister read. Having dreams was one thing, but Anastasia almost always went overboard with her fanciful imagination. Men like the ones in her stories simply didn't exist.

The bell above the front door jingled, and Charlotte looked up with a start, her breath catching in her throat. Anastasia even had *her* anticipating Mr. Baxton's arrival. A moment later, she exhaled. "Good morning, Mr. Read," she said, greeting one of her regular customers. "Have you finished the *Canterbury Tales* already?"

The diminutive, slender man doffed his top hat and tucked it under one arm, revealing his custoLaura center-parted hairstyle, the honey-gold strands pressed close to his head. "Good afternoon, Miss Pringle." He offered a congenial smile. "As a matter of fact, I have. I must confess, I found the Miller's Tale to be the most enjoyable. *And* I've come seeking another treasure, hoping you might point me in the right direction. Your recommendation was spot on, and I have no doubt you'll do the same again." He winked.

Charlotte smiled in return. What Mr. Read lacked in stature, he made up for in social graces and personality. And his two sons, not long in their britches, were already showing signs of growing up to be just like their father.

"If you found Mr. Chaucer's storytelling to your liking, you should next read the stories of Grendel and Beowulf." She led Mr. Read down the first aisle, running her fingers across the titles and moving just a little beyond another copy of Chaucer's tales to retrieve a book. "Beowulf is a hero of the Geats and battles against Grendel, Grendel's mother, and a dragon, then becomes king of the Geats. It's an epic poem I am certain you will find engaging."

Mr. Read held the book in his hands and glanced at the cover. He ran his fingers over the title, and then he opened the book to the first few pages. Moments later, he closed the cover and looked up at Charlotte. "I shall take it." He gestured for her to precede him back up the aisle toward the front, continuing as he followed. "Under normal circumstances, I would preview an unfamiliar text before purchasing, but I know you would not steer me wrong." He reached for his billfold then paused. "Oh, and while I am here, might you also have something I could read to my sons? The tales penned by Chaucer fair well enough, but I fear Beowulf's story might be a bit beyond them."

"Of course." Charlotte nodded and looked toward her sister. "Anastasia, would you mind pulling two or three of Hans Christian Andersen's fairy tales for Mr. Read, please?"

"Right away." Her sister disappeared down the far aisle and returned moments later. Having someone else who knew the bookshop well was a definite asset. "Here you are." Anastasia set the three books on the counter with the other.

Mr. Read bestowed a pleased grin on Anastasia. "Thank you, my dear." He glanced at the titles and read them aloud. "*The Steadfast Tin Soldier, The Ugly Duckling*, and *The Emperor's New Clothes*." With a nod, he pushed the stack toward Charlotte. "These shall do nicely." After laying his hat on the counter, he retrieved his billfold, withdrew a few bills and some change, and paid for his purchases.

"Thank you again, Mr. Read." Charlotte noted the titles on her inventory ledger and slid the stack back toward him.

"No, thank *you*, Miss Pringle." He nodded toward Anastasia. "And to the younger Miss Pringle, as well." Taking the books and setting his hat atop his head, he bowed toward them both. "It is the endless hours of enjoyment you provide with your bookshop that is the greater gift. My dear wife, sons, and I all appreciate your service." With a tip of his hat, he left the shop, the door jingling the bell with his departure.

"I'm glad I was here to see Mr. Read," Anastasia remarked as soon as the door closed. The two sisters watched the street outside as their recent customer crossed to the park on the other side and disappeared from view. "He is one of your nicest customers."

"I cannot disagree with you, although Mrs. Merriweather and Miss Constance are among my most loyal."

Anastasia giggled. "And most talkative."

"This is true." Charlotte smiled. "Let's not forget the brooding Mr. Cramer, with his dark eyes and pinched lips."

Warming to the little game, her sister brightened. "Or the pensive and serious Mrs. Standish. Every time I see her, I wonder if she knows what a smile is." A twinkle lit Anastasia's eyes as a teasing grin formed on her lips. "And what about Mr. Charles du Pont II? He seems to enjoy frequenting this bookshop, although it's curious how often he leaves without making a purchase." She tapped her index finger to her pursed lips. "I wonder what it is that appeals to him so much about this little shop."

"Mr. Charles du Pont is charming, I agree." Charlotte raised one eyebrow. "But have you not also noticed how often he walks in the park across the street with Miss Amelia on his arm? Besides"—Charlotte returned her sister's teasing grin—"I happen to believe Thomas and Alfred du Pont present a much better diversion and are far better topics of conversation."

A telltale blush stole into Anastasia's cheeks as the young girl dipped her head. She clasped her hands in front of her, her gaze fastened to the floor. Just as Charlotte expected. Her sister couldn't deny the way those two young lads doted on her every word or how often they went out of their way to catch a glimpse of her in the shop. Charlotte had lost count of how many times they walked by the windows, pretending not to look inside. At least they came from good families. Father couldn't fault their lineage, nor the powder mills their family operated along the banks of the Brandywine. It was the only reason Charlotte encouraged the antics. She had to look out for her sister's interests, after all.

Further banter was interrupted by the jingle of the bell. Anastasia retrieved the duster and returned to her work, leaving Charlotte to greet their new customer. Her sister could be quite adept at disappearing. With a glance at the front door, Charlotte was surprised to see a dark-haired gentleman backing into the shop, his shoulders slightly hunched and his hip pushing against the door as if he was pulling something heavy.

She immediately rushed from behind the counter to lend her assistance but froze when the man maneuvered his way beyond the door and pivoted to face her. His long fingers wrapped around the handles of a wheeled chair carrying a young girl who looked to be about ten or eleven years old. A top hat sat on top of a blanket that rested across her legs and covered most of her simple yet stylish black frock.

Charlotte didn't often see an apparatus such as this, and her imagination immediately began to form several stories to explain the background she envisioned for her two visitors.

Charlotte shook her head and remembered her manners. She stepped forward as the gentleman's smooth cocoa gaze met hers. His breath came in labored yet measured spurts, but his expression held no sign of weariness or strain.

"Welcome to Cobblestone Books, sir. I am Miss Pringle, the owner. How may we be of service this morning?"

Surprise flickered in the gentleman's eyes as he tilted his head a fraction of an inch. He glanced around the shop then turned his attention to Charlotte. Stepping around the wheeled chair, whose occupant observed Charlotte with pensive curiosity, the gentleman placed one hand on the lapels of his overcoat. "Miss Pringle, I am Mr. Baxton. We have exchanged correspondence regarding my visit." Extending a hand toward her, he waited for her to return the gesture before continuing. "It is a pleasure to make your acquaintance," he said as he bowed over her hand, his mouth hovering just a hair's breadth above her knuckles.

With her hand tucked back against the folds of her skirts, Charlotte forced herself to reconcile the image she'd had of Mr. Baxton with the reality standing before her. Snippets of her sister's earlier repartee came to mind, but she brushed them aside.

Business. The single word served to set her thoughts straight again. A customer needed her help. She must remain focused. Never mind if the man's angled jaw line and high cheekbones gave him an air of distinction.

"Yes, yes, of course, Mr. Baxton. It is a pleasure to meet you as well."

He placed a hand on the young girl's shoulder and smiled. "Allow me to introduce my charming yet precocious niece, Grace Baxton." With a glance down at the blue-eyed girl, he winked and looked up again at Charlotte. "It is for her that we have journeyed to your shop. She has read every book in my possession, and we are in dire need of additional stories to keep her occupied."

Grace swatted at her uncle and gave him a stern yet amused stare. "That is not true, Uncle Richard. There are lots more books on the shelves in your library. But those are boring. You can have those."

Charlotte held back a grin at the girl's forthrightness then stepped forward and extended her right hand. "Grace, I am honored to meet you. And I'm very happy you have chosen my bookshop to satisfy your insatiable love of reading."

Grace shook Charlotte's hand and dipped slightly forward, as close to a curtsey as she could no doubt perform. "It's a pleasure, Miss Pringle." She tilted her tawny-haired head and scrunched her eyebrows together, two lines forming at the center. "What's *insatiable*?" she asked, sounding out each syllable.

"It means you have a love of reading that knows no end."

"Oh." The girl nodded. "Yes. That's true. I just love books. So many stories. So much adventure." A dreamy expression crossed her face. "I could get lost for hours."

Charlotte winked. "I know exactly what you mean."

Grace beamed at the shared understanding. Then her attention shifted to somewhere over Charlotte's shoulder. "Who's that?"

Charlotte glanced behind her. So much for remembering her manners. "Oh, that is my sister." She beckoned Anastasia with a wave of her hand. "Anastasia, I'd like you to meet Mr. Baxton and his niece Grace." Once her sister was at her side, Charlotte shifted her focus to the other pair. "Mr. Baxton, Grace, this is Anastasia Pringle."

Anastasia dipped into a quick curtsey. "Pleased to meet you both."

"My sister often spends her spare time with me, keeping the shop clean and shelving new books I've acquired. She also helps with customer purchases and is a tremendous assistant. I don't know what I would do without her."

Her sister bent low and leaned toward Grace, answering in a loud whisper. "Don't let my sister fool you. Charlotte and I have a lot of fun."

Grace giggled, and Anastasia straightened. "Would you like to come with me and take a tour of the shop?" She looked to Mr. Baxton and gestured toward the handles of the wheeled chair. "May I?"

Mr. Baxton hesitated, but at Grace's eager nod, he relinquished control and stepped back. "Grace can maneuver quite well on her own, too. Don't allow her to get lazy."

Anastasia led Grace away, chattering with the younger girl as they began their tour. Charlotte addressed Mr. Baxton. "The books you requested are here. I believe I found each and every one." She retrieved the small stack from behind the counter and placed it on top. Mr. Baxton closed the distance in three long steps. "Of course, you are under no obligation to purchase them all. I merely wanted to have them on hand for your perusal."

Mr. Baxton reached out and picked up each book in turn, holding them in his hands, turning them over, and flipping through the first few pages. He recognized the value of books. Charlotte could see that in the way he handled them. As he set the last book on top of the stack, he nodded. His expression reflected satisfaction. "They're in excellent condition."

Pride brought a smile to Charlotte's lips. "I insist that my books remain in the best form possible. Books available for purchase are guaranteed brand-new, and those available for borrowing are of the highest quality. If a book becomes tattered or torn, I do what I can to restore it, but if it is beyond repair, I offer it for sale at a lower price to anyone who wishes to purchase it. I also sell a few antique titles."

"Sounds perfectly reasonable. It's no wonder you have established a reputation that has spread as far as Ashbourne Hills, although I have a feeling knowledge of your shop extends further than that." Mr. Baxton glanced over his shoulder toward the doors. "And you couldn't have found a more perfect location. Customers can come here to acquire a book then venture to the park where they can relax and read." He turned back to face her with a twinkle in his eyes. "A winning combination."

Charlotte couldn't help responding to his congenial manner. A pleasant feeling sent warmth flowing through her veins. "It *has* proven to be good for business."

Mr. Baxton placed one well-manicured hand on top of the stack of books. These were not the hands of a common laborer, though the small scars and scrapes bore evidence of some form of work. "I'm pleased to hear that. Too many bookshops are forced to close their doors because of lack of business." He sighed. "Often, it's due to location. Other times, it's because the proprietor"—he gave her an acknowledging nod—"or proprietress doesn't truly love what he or she does. That's why my niece and I traveled here from Ashbourne Hills." He wrapped both hands around the books. "Well, I don't want to keep you any longer than necessary. How much do I owe you?"

Charlotte stated the total amount, and Mr. Baxton paid without hesitation. She procured a burlap sack and slid his books inside.

"I suppose it's time for us to depart. That is, if my niece will be willing to leave," he said with a wink. "Grace?"

"Yes, Uncle Richard?" The voice came from the back corner of the store, opposite where they stood.

"I have your books, and it is time for us to take our leave."

"Aw, Uncle Richard. Do we have to go so soon?"

Charlotte could almost picture the pouty lips and the woeful expression on the girl's face.

"I promise we shall return soon. Besides, you have a great deal of reading to do. We need to go home so you can get started."

Anastasia poked her head around a corner of one of the shelves. Grace appeared a moment later. Wheeling herself to the front of the store, Grace joined her uncle at the counter.

"All right. I'm ready to go." She crossed her arms. "But you must know how much I protest this departure."

Mr. Baxton turned to Charlotte, his mouth pressed into a thin line as he held back his laughter. With the sack held securely in his left hand, he extended his right. The warmth in his long fingers as they enveloped her own threatened to send a shiver up her back. But she resisted. Instead, she took a deep breath as he bowed slightly and raised her hand toward his lips.

"We shall return. You have my word on that." Mr. Baxton released her hand and stepped behind Grace. He placed the sack of books in her lap then positioned his hands on the wheeled chair. "Thank you again for your time, Miss Pringle. It has been a distinct pleasure."

As they reached the entrance, Mr. Baxton grabbed the door, but Anastasia beat him to it. She held it open, and Mr. Baxton backed Grace out to the sidewalk. He replaced his hat then touched two fingers to the brim in farewell, and before Charlotte knew it, the pair disappeared from view.

Charlotte stared out the bowed-front window, not seeing anything. It took several moments to realize her sister was speaking to her. She turned with a start.

"I'm sorry, Anastasia, what did you say?"

Her sister narrowed her eyes in silent assessment. "I said Grace is an amazing girl. I don't know if I could be as good-natured as she is if I were the one confined to a chair all day. But I like her." She raised one brow. "And her uncle seemed rather taken with you, as well."

Uh-oh. Charlotte recognized that look in her sister's eyes. It meant only one thing. Trouble. She'd better put a stop to things before any more ideas started stirring in that fanciful mind Anastasia possessed.

"Mr. Baxton was very cordial."

"Cordial?" Both eyebrows raised. "That's all you're willing to admit?"

Charlotte shrugged. "He was here only for a brief visit. What more could I possibly say about him? We didn't exactly have long to converse."

"Grace and I had the same amount of time, and I learned all about the accident that led to her being in the wheeled chair, how she came to live with her uncle, and the hope she has to one day walk again." She crossed her arms and glowered. "If she and I can talk about all of that, you and her uncle should have been able to discuss at least that much."

"Well, we primarily spoke of the bookshop and of Grace's love of reading. There truly wasn't time for much else."

"But he did promise to return. So maybe you can do better next time."

"Better?" Charlotte gave her sister a wry grin. "Are you insinuating I did a poor job with this conversation?"

Anastasia took a step back and held up her hands. "No, not at all. You were likely your usual self, keeping all talk to the bookshop, books, and reading."

"And what else is there to discuss when a customer comes in to shop?"

"Well, you could share a little about yourself."

"With someone I've just met? I wouldn't be so presumptuous."

Her sister sighed and rolled her eyes. "You're hopeless."

"No," Charlotte countered. "Merely practical." She had such fun baiting her sister and playing to her conniving, matchmaking schemes. But the last thing she needed was a young girl interfering with her customers.

"And that will never secure you a man," her sister said under her breath.

"What was that?"

Anastasia jerked up her head. "I said, uh, as the owner, I can understand."

Charlotte closed her eyes and shook her head. Some days, her sister could try her nerves. But most of the time having Anastasia at the shop brightened Charlotte's day.

"All right." Charlotte clapped her hands together. "What do you say we close up for lunch and a walk in the park?"

"I would love it!"

"You retrieve our lunches, and let Laura know it's time for a break."

Once on the cobblestone sidewalk, Charlotte turned the key in the lock and pivoted to stand beside her sister. She glanced up and down the busy street. Although she'd deny it, her thoughts dwelled on Mr. Baxton and his niece. A slow grin formed. She looked over her shoulder at the front of her shop, wondering when she would see them again.

⁊⸘

"How did your day go, Charlotte?" Her mother took the seat Father held out for her in their formal dining room. "Did you have many customers?"

Charlotte took her seat across from her mother. She had arrived home with barely enough time to dress for dinner. The rich aromas of braised beef and au gratin potatoes teased her nose. "It seemed to be a typical day by all accounts. I had a handful of my customers who frequent the shop on a regular basis." Her stomach rumbled, and she swallowed, anticipating the delicious meal about to be served.

"And one new one," Anastasia added. "Or two, if you count his niece. I am certain they will become regular customers before long."

The older of her two younger sisters stared at Charlotte in surprise. "You never told me about this." Bethany leaned in close and lowered her voice. "I shall expect a full report once dinner is completed."

"New customers are always good," Father said, leaning to allow the staff ample room to serve the meal.

Charlotte smiled and spoke a low "thank you" to Fiona as the girl served her. The young girl bobbed a curtsey and continued in silence. "Yes," Charlotte replied. "A great number of new patrons have visited my shop in the past few weeks. If this continues, I might have to consider hiring an additional assistant. Laura is quite adept, but I am not certain she is free to work to that capacity."

Father extended his hands toward his wife and Charlotte. "Shall we bless the meal?"

Charlotte joined hands with Bethany, and Anastasia took their mother's hand as Father said grace. The table was far too wide to complete the circle. Not like when Devon still lived with them. Some days it felt like mere days instead of four months since he'd married and moved out. Charlotte missed his teasing, jovial presence but missed her big brother's counsel and protectiveness more. So much now fell on her shoulders. She didn't know if she could handle it. Bethany filled part of the void with her level-headed advice. It wasn't the same, though.

Once grace had been said, Mother took a sip of water and dabbed her lips. "Perhaps you could allow that assistant to assume more of your responsibilities," she said, continuing the earlier conversation. "It would free you to pursue other interests rather than spend all your time in that dusty shop."

"Or take walks in the park should a certain gentleman ask." Anastasia patted her stylish blond curls and batted her eyelashes.

"Shush," Charlotte reprimanded her sister, narrowing her

eyes and leveling a glare her way. The girl could be absolutely incorrigible.

"So Anastasia has met this gentleman, yet you neglect to share such important information with me?" Bethany gave a dramatic sigh. "I see where I rank in matters of importance."

"Bethany, it isn't like that at all," Charlotte protested. "Anastasia simply happened to be present when he arrived this afternoon. Had she not, it is likely neither one of you would be aware of him."

Father raised one eyebrow and regarded his three daughters. "It seems this gentleman has made quite an impact on all three of you." He cut a sliver of beef then stabbed it with his fork and paused before raising it to his mouth. "But you need to mind your manners and save your squabbles for the drawing room or your private chambers."

"Yes, Father."

"I'm sorry, Father."

The girls all nodded their dutiful obedience. Bethany nudged Charlotte, and they both shared a private grin with Anastasia across the table. This conversation would definitely continue later.

A few moments of silence ensued before Mother cleared her throat. "Does this gentleman have a name?"

Charlotte patted her mouth and returned her napkin to her lap. "Mr. Richard Baxton."

Mother's eyes widened. "Of the Ashbourne Hills Baxtons?"

"And Baxton Shipping?" Father added.

"I'm not certain." Charlotte furrowed her brow and tilted her head. "We did not speak much about personal matters during his brief visit." She recalled the return address on his letter. "Oh, but I do believe he *does* live in Ashbourne Hills."

Mother looked at Father. "Is that not the family who has recently suffered the loss of one of its sons?"

Father stroked his slightly graying moustache and beard. "If this gentleman is indeed from the family who owns Baxton Shipping, then yes." He looked again at Charlotte. "Did he not mention anything today that might confirm this?"

"Oh, it must be!" Anastasia jumped in. "I spoke with his niece this afternoon, and she told me about her recent accident. She was in a wheeled chair, too!"

"Anastasia." Father's low warning served its purpose.

"I'm sorry, Father." Anastasia lapsed into instant silence.

"Anastasia is correct," Charlotte continued. "Mr. Baxton's niece Grace was with him today. And she was in a rather ornate wheeled chair." She sipped her water. "It would seem this is the same Baxton family of which you and Mother have heard."

"Not only heard, Charlotte," Father countered. "We have engaged in business dealings with Baxton Shipping on more than one occasion, supplying gunpowder barrels for some of their ships over the years. Your Mother and I have also attended one or two social events at one of their homes."

What a small world. Charlotte could hardly believe a man who this afternoon seemed to be completely disconnected from her life had turned out to be entwined with her family's business.

Mother glanced across the table and caught Charlotte's eye. "If this Mr. Baxton becomes a regular customer, we shall have to invite him to join us one evening for dinner."

"Yes," Father agreed. "I would like to discuss a few business matters with him, and we will be sure to have Devon and his wife join us, too."

Charlotte's excitement over this potential friendship dimmed a little at the prospect of Mr. Baxton spending time in their home. That was the way things were done, but she had secretly hoped to have him to herself to some extent. . .at least at the bookshop. Then again, having him involved with her family could prove advantageous. She would have to wait and see.

three

The bell above the shop door jingled, and Charlotte looked up, her breath catching in her throat. A second later, her shoulders slumped.

Foolishness. Utter foolishness.

It had been nearly two weeks since Mr. Baxton and his niece had left her shop, promising to return. Her head told her it was too soon. Despite Grace's obvious love of reading, her uncle had purchased four books. It took time to read that many books. And the girl most likely had daily studies, as well. Charlotte felt guilty for expecting to see them so soon, but she couldn't persuade her mind and heart to react otherwise.

"Good afternoon, Mr. Couper." He might not be the man she hoped to see, but at least she could enjoy visiting with one of her regular patrons.

"Ah, good afternoon, Miss Pringle." The elderly gentleman removed his top hat, his ornate walking cane preceding him by one step. "And how are you on this grand and fortuitous day?"

He certainly seemed in a much brighter mood than normal. Charlotte could use an infusion of cheer to offset her disappointment.

"I am quite well, thank you. Have you received good news recently?"

A gleam in his eyes accompanied a teasing grin on his lips. "Why do you ask?" He was baiting her. She knew it.

"As much as I would like to believe otherwise, I can hardly imagine your enthusiasm is reserved solely for the joy of coming to this shop and finding another book to read."

"Touché," he countered. "Although I must correct you on one point. I do enjoy discovering new books. So my delight is partially reserved for my visits here every other week." Pressing his index finger to the counter in front of her, he fixed his reprimanding glance on her. "Do have more confidence in the appeal of this quaint shop. You have no idea how many lives you are impacting, nor how many pleased customers you are serving."

Chagrin filled her. "You are right, Mr. Couper. I shall endeavor to remember that in the future." She lightly grasped the edge of the counter with her fingers. "Now, do tell me about this good news. Then we can see about finding a new book for you."

"If you insist," he said with a mock sigh. Tucking his hat under his arm, he assumed a stance similar to one about to give a great speech. "You are familiar with the gardens adjoining my home on the Strand."

"Oh yes. I don't venture south to New Castle often, but when I am there, I always stroll along the cobblestone streets and marvel at the unique architecture of the homes. Yours stands sentinel over the Delaware River in a magnificent manner."

"Thank you. I quite agree, although I certainly can't presume to take credit for the beauty of its architecture. That honor distinctly belongs to Mr. George Read II. After his son passed away and the fire in town damaged so many homes, my brother was fortunate to acquire the land at public auction. Together, we repaired the damaged areas and created the formal gardens adjacent to the house."

"So those weren't always a part of the property?"

"No. From what I gather, when it was built, the focus was only on the stately and rather expansive home. Mr. Read spared no expense, right down to the silver-plated doorknobs."

Charlotte covered her mouth and giggled. Such extravagance. Then again, from what she'd heard and read about Mr. Read, profligacy and excessive behavior were apt descriptions.

"I recently hired a gardener to bring a fresh, new look to the various trees and flower beds," Mr. Couper continued. "He suggested adding one or two fountains and perhaps a few benches along a brick walking path. I hear tell he even spent time working for Joshua and Samuel Peirce on Peirce's Park."

"Oh! I adore that park. The gardens and fountains are beautiful." Charlotte nodded toward the park across the street. "As much as I enjoy time spent right here, there is something special about those gardens. They are no doubt the most beautiful in all of the Brandywine Valley. The Peirce brothers obviously had a deep love for the arboretum they planted."

"Yes, and it being open to public viewing enhances its beauty and appeal."

"So when is this renovation set to commence?"

"I am not certain, but I believe within the month."

"The next time I am in New Castle, I shall be certain to pay a visit and see the results of this gardener's handiwork."

Mr. Couper rapped his cane on the floor, the impact making a muffled thump against the woven carpet on which he stood. "Yes, you must. And tell me," he directed, glancing about to the left and right, "where is that charming little sister of yours? I don't believe I've seen her walking about the shop today."

"No, she isn't here this afternoon. She's working on a special project with two other students from her school. This is her last year, and she wants to finish with top honors."

"If she is anything like her older sister, I am certain she will," Mr. Couper said. "Now, let us talk about the real reason for my visit today."

Charlotte smiled. Mr. Couper always had some story to tell or news to report whenever he paid a visit. Some might find his eccentric ways a bother, but she enjoyed his company. He always returned the books he borrowed in excellent condition and had been a loyal customer almost since the day she opened her doors.

"So," Charlotte began, "what type of literature would you like to explore this time?"

"Actually"—he hooked his cane over his arm and turned toward the shelves behind him—"I'm here for my two grandsons. They have been creating their own adventures for some time now, and I'd like them to take a few adventures through books. What do you have that might appeal to them?"

"I know just where to direct you." Charlotte led Mr. Couper toward the shelves marked for younger readers. Locating the section she was seeking, she explained, "Just about anything written by Mark Twain, Jules Verne, or Lewis Carroll will be perfect for them."

Mr. Couper stepped closer to the shelves, and Charlotte moved to give him more room.

"I'll leave you to peruse these titles. If you have any questions, don't hesitate to ask."

"Thank you," he said without looking up, his eagerness keeping his attention locked on the books.

Charlotte continued the rest of the way up the aisle and heard the bell above the front door jingle just as she stepped into the open section of her shop. Stopping to straighten a few books on one of her feature displays, she didn't see her latest customer until he spoke.

"Good afternoon, Miss Pringle."

Mr. Baxton's voice was like warm, velvety chocolate being poured over vanilla ice cream. Charlotte tried to remain calm and professional, but she knew a silly grin had formed on her lips, and she couldn't will it away.

"Good afternoon, Mr. Baxton. I'm happy to see you have returned." Excited, eager, and relieved might be more accurate. At least now she could stop watching the door every minute. "But aren't you missing someone?" Charlotte looked behind him as if Grace might be waiting outside.

Mr. Baxton moved the scarf that hung around his neck to the side and unbuttoned the top two buttons of his overcoat. "Yes, I wasn't able to bring my niece with me today. She had an appointment with a specialist in Philadelphia that will last for most of the day. My mother, her grandmother, is with her, overseeing the appointment, so I decided now would be an excellent time to return. That way, I can have a surprise for her when I meet her after she's done."

The obvious affection he held for his niece touched a special place in Charlotte's heart.

"I'm certain she will be overcome with joy when she sees what you've brought. Now if you don't mind my asking, how did you come to be Grace's caretaker and guardian? And please don't hesitate to tell me if I'm being presumptuous. My curious nature often goes several steps ahead of my better judgment."

Mr. Baxton chuckled, alleviating Charlotte's concerns. "I don't mind talking about it. . .at least not now. Two months ago, my reaction would have been quite different. But time does allow the pain to heal." He moved toward one of the front tables and perched on the edge. His eyes took on a faraway look. With a deep breath, he began. "Grace was in a carriage with my brother and his wife. The carriage hit a deep rut in the road, causing one of the axles to break. It spooked the horses, and they bolted, broken axle and all."

A soft gasp escaped Charlotte's lips, but Mr. Baxton didn't seem to notice. He barely broke his stride in the retelling, seemingly lost in the memories.

"Elliott tried to persuade his wife and daughter to jump to

safety ahead of him, but just as he managed to get the door open, the carriage careened over the edge of a fairly steep drop-off. Grace was thrown clear, but Elliott and Constance were trapped inside."

Charlotte closed her eyes against the horrific images his words created. How completely awful for Grace to have to endure something like that. And for Mr. Baxton, too.

"My brother and his wife didn't survive the crash, and as you have seen, Grace suffers from paralysis of the legs."

To lose a brother and a sister-in-law and then to become the sole caretaker of an injured niece—Charlotte could barely fathom the shock. Yet Mr. Baxton appeared to have adjusted rather well. And Grace obviously adored him. Respect for the man increased tenfold.

"You mentioned an appointment with a specialist today. So I assume the doctors haven't determined if Grace's injury is permanent?"

Mr. Baxton ran a hand through his hair, making a few stubborn locks stick out and one curl fall below his well-styled hairline. "No." He sighed. "And we have seen far too many, if you ask me. I have a hard time being patient when doctors who are supposed to have answers don't have any to offer me." A growl escaped his lips. "And Grace. It's not easy seeing the hope spark in her eyes with each new specialist we see, only to witness it being snuffed out like the gas streetlamps every morning at dawn. I don't know how much more of this I can take."

Charlotte tried to put herself in his shoes, tried to imagine what it might be like if she were the sole caretaker of a child such as Grace. Would she be able to handle it as well as Mr. Baxton apparently did? He still struggled. Anyone would. But the fact that he accepted the responsibility thrust at him spoke volumes. A lesser man would have walked away.

"And. . ." Charlotte began, uncertain if she should proceed.

"Yes?" Mr. Baxton replied, his tone and expression encouraging her to continue.

"And other children? Did Grace have any brothers or sisters?"

"No." He sighed. His eyes held such sadness. "Elliott and Constance. . ." He stopped, appearing to rethink what he was about to say. "No, there weren't," he finally said.

Charlotte wanted to reach out and cover his hands with her own, but she didn't want to overstep the bounds of propriety. Instead, she put all her sympathy into her voice, hoping her eyes conveyed what physical touch couldn't. "I truly am sorry for your loss. You and Grace both." She placed her hands on the countertop and leaned forward. "I have a feeling God has something very special planned for that little girl."

"Yes," he said, regarding her with a curious expression. He tugged on the two ends of his scarf. "I admit it's difficult trying to figure out why God would allow something so tragic to happen to such an innocent little girl. And there have been times I haven't been the best role model for Grace," he added with a rueful grin.

"Anyone in your circumstances would react the same way. And given the situation, I would say you are entitled to a few weak moments." If it had been her, Charlotte would have had more than her fair share of weak moments.

One side of Mr. Baxton's mouth turned up. The first sign their conversation was taking a lighter turn. "Why, thank you, Miss Pringle. It is a comfort to know you understand."

Charlotte held up one hand. "I am not certain I understand, as much as I can sympathize with what you're facing." She clasped her hands tightly, offered what she hoped was an air of lightheartedness, and prayed he wouldn't consider it inappropriate. "It seems all those books I've read haven't been for naught."

The genuine smile he'd worn when he first entered her shop returned. "You are correct. And whether it's empathy or sympathy"—he stood and bestowed upon her a formal bow, his eyes twinkling as his gaze met hers—"I shall take either one. I make no qualms about particulars."

Relaxing her grip, Charlotte exhaled slowly and quietly. She often couldn't determine when the right moment came to interject a little humor, especially when the conversation leading up to that point had been melancholy. But Mr. Baxton didn't seem to mind, and now they could move beyond the unpleasant memories of his recent loss.

"So." Mr. Baxton's voice interrupted her musings. "Now that you know all about my recent state of affairs, what do you say we discuss the object of those affairs and locate a few more books to help Grace pass the time?"

Charlotte shifted her focus and became a bookshop owner once more. It wouldn't be easy treating Mr. Baxton as just another customer, but she'd see to his needs and allow him to take the lead.

"Yes, of course." She joined him in front of the counter as they faced the aisles and shelves of books. "I recall the books you purchased on your last visit. But they contained a wide variety of stories and writing styles. Why don't you tell me the types of things Grace likes? Then we shall see which of the many books will suit her interests best."

He nodded. "Sounds logical." Mr. Baxton cocked his head. "Let me see. I know she loved this book about island adventures, but I don't recall the title or the author."

Charlotte mentally scanned the list of titles she could bring to mind. "Could it be *The Swiss Family Robinson* by Johann David Wyss?"

Mr. Baxton snapped his fingers. "Yes! That's the one. She spoke endlessly of it for days. I almost felt I was right there with the family by the time Grace found another book to capture her attention."

Charlotte jotted down the title on a piece of paper. "Books do have a way of doing that to a person." She spoke from experience. She couldn't recall the number of times her parents had had to reprimand her and tell her to focus on her studies more than her pleasure reading. They of course had been right, and now that her school days were behind her, Charlotte could read to her heart's content.

"All right," Mr. Baxton continued, "we have that one book as an example. But Grace also loves reading about faraway places and adores the stories where the princess must be rescued by the handsome prince."

"What girl doesn't? You never outgrow that tale," Charlotte said without thinking, as she wrote down a few more notes.

"It doesn't always have to be a fairy tale," he said softly.

Charlotte glanced up to see a wry grin on Mr. Baxton's lips and a teasing twinkle in his eyes. She was tempted to allow a glimpse of her own dreams and desires but instead chose the safe and impersonal route. "You are correct. It is a timeless story that manifests itself in a variety of ways through many different lives. Just when you start to believe the happily-ever-after is out of reach, the prince makes an appearance and a satisfying conclusion is reached."

"Which brings me to another favorite of Grace's. She cannot seem to get enough of the stories about fighting against seemingly impossible odds and winning. It's what gives me hope that her paralysis won't become a permanent part of her life."

Charlotte touched the unsharpened end of the pencil to her chin. "I have only spoken to Grace the one time, and I certainly don't know her as well as you, but she doesn't appear to be a girl who gives up easily." She pointed the pencil in Mr. Baxton's direction. "I can imagine how exhausting the visits to the specialists can become. And if she loves those stories about impossible odds, she will find a way to win over her circumstances."

He nodded. "You are correct. Despite the repetitive cycle of disappointing news or no answers at all, Grace's determination is what keeps me fighting for her."

Once again, she pointed the pencil toward Mr. Baxton. "You are a constant source of strength for your niece. Do not forget that a champion for the handsome prince is just as important in the battle as the actual fight the prince must endure."

"True."

Charlotte straightened and picked up the pad of paper. "I think I have enough information to make some recommendations."

A few minutes later, Mr. Baxton followed Charlotte to the front, his arms laden with copies of *Ivanhoe*, *Oliver Twist*, *Nicholas Nickleby*, *The Three Musketeers*, and *Alice's Adventures in Wonderland*. He quickly paid for his purchases and waited while Charlotte placed them in a sack.

"Once again," he said as he tipped his imaginary hat, "I am in your debt. Grace will be beside herself when I collect her from the specialist's office and present her with these surprises."

"And once again, it is my pleasure. I look forward to hearing how she liked these and which one was her favorite." Perhaps Mr. Baxton would bring Grace again so the little girl could answer for herself. Charlotte wouldn't mind seeing either one of them again.

After buttoning the top buttons of his overcoat, Mr. Baxton tucked the sack against him with his left arm and bowed over her hand. "Miss Pringle, I bid you good day and offer my deepest appreciation for your time."

"You are most welcome, Mr. Baxton." He held her gaze a moment longer, and Charlotte swallowed in an attempt to calm her erratic heartbeat. "Good day," she managed, although her voice sounded forced to her own ears.

He turned and headed for the door, casting one final look over his shoulder and waving as he left the shop.

"Now, that man fancies you. There's no doubt about it."

Startled by Mr. Couper's voice, Charlotte turned with a jolt to face him. He wore a wide grin as he stood supported by his walking cane.

"And judging from the bits of conversation I heard, I believe the attraction is reciprocated."

Warmth crept up Charlotte's neck, and she took a deep breath in an attempt to prevent it from reaching her face. "Shame on you, Mr. Couper, for eavesdropping," she said without irritation. "You were supposed to be looking for books for your grandsons."

"But I was," he countered, holding up three titles. "And I have found them." He walked to the counter, his expression one of pure mischief. "Can you truly fault a man who merely wishes happiness for his favorite bookshop owner?"

Charlotte pursed her lips and regarded the gentleman. How could she possibly be cross with him? In many ways, he reminded her of her father. He'd even told her on more than one occasion that he'd never had a daughter. She certainly couldn't begrudge him some harmless banter.

"All right, Mr. Couper, I shall forgive you. . .this time," she said with a grin.

"Ah," he sighed as he ran his fingers over his well-groomed mustache, "if only I could be here when that young gentleman returns." He winked. "I should like to hear the reason he gives for prolonging his stay."

"You, Mr. Couper, are up to no good."

"I wouldn't have it any other way, Miss Pringle."

She obviously wasn't going to win this argument, so she should probably redirect their conversation. "Shall I total your purchases for you?"

He placed the three books on the counter and nodded. "If

you must."

She gave him the amount, and he counted out the coins.

With the three books in one hand and his cane in the other, he sauntered to the door. "I expect to hear about Mr. Baxton's return and perhaps even his niece when I next visit your shop."

"I will do my best to oblige."

Mr. Couper pointed his cane at her. "See that you do, young lady." Tipping his hat, he took his leave.

Charlotte leaned back against the shelf behind her and smiled. Days like this one made being a bookshop owner a true delight.

four

"Mr. Baxton, might I have a word with you?"

The doctor summoned Richard from the waiting room, where he and Mother sat, as a dark-haired nurse escorted Grace out from an examining room. The woman's stark white uniform blended almost too well with the white-painted walls and immaculate marble floors.

"Grace, I will only keep your uncle for a moment. I am sure your grandmother will be more than happy to continue keeping you company." The doctor gave Grace and Mother a kind smile, compassion reflecting in his eyes. He turned to Richard and gestured toward the room Grace just left. "If you please, Mr. Baxton?"

Richard preceded the doctor into the room and waited while the man closed the door. He'd been in a number of similar rooms, but this one possessed a warmth he'd not felt in any of the others. The color of the walls, the furniture, and the various items on the table welcomed anyone entering.

"Will you have a seat?"

Richard took one of the two cushioned chairs opposite the doctor's desk and was surprised when the doctor took the other. The man reached for a folder on the edge of his desk and flipped it open.

"I promised your niece I would only keep you for a moment, Mr. Baxton, and I intend to keep my word."

"So what is the prognosis?" Richard wasn't in the mood to waste any time. "Grace and I have been through this several times. If what you have to say isn't encouraging, we might as well get right to it."

The specialist sighed. "I know how tiring this must be for you both. But I am glad you came to see me. As you are aware, I have done extensive research and study on the subject of paralysis. Your niece's case is not unique."

Richard moved to the edge of the seat. "Do you mean you have seen this before?"

"Yes, and I have seen it cured, as well."

Finally! Richard's heart beat faster. At long last, they might have some good news. Of course the doctor hadn't exactly said anything one way or another.

The doctor held up a hand of caution. "I do not want what I am about to say to be construed in the wrong manner. But based upon my examination of your niece and her response to some of the more detailed tests, she has a chance at walking again."

"A chance? Does that mean there is also a chance she might not walk again?"

"Correct. The odds are as much in Grace's favor as they are against her. But it's going to take a lot of hard work on Grace's part, as well as yours."

"We are no strangers to hard work, Doctor. I can assure you of that." Richard pressed his palms to his knees. "Ever since the accident, we have worked daily on exercises, both of us hoping it would do some good and that one day we'd start to see results. When I am unavailable to assist, her grandmother helps in my place." Those exercises hadn't been easy. It nearly broke his heart to see his niece struggle so often. Not to mention how hard she tried with seemingly no improvement.

"You and your mother are to be commended, Mr. Baxton. Those very exercises can be credited with putting your niece in such a favorable position. Unfortunately, the dedication of many of the patients I see isn't nearly as serious, nor are they as determined as the three of you obviously have been." The doctor consulted his notes, flipping through several pages. "Because you have remained faithful in exercising even when you haven't seen evidence of it making any difference, Grace's muscle tone and reflexes have remained strong. Far too often, I witness atrophy of the muscles and no sign whatsoever of any reflexive response. For those patients, my prognosis isn't as encouraging. Now, Grace does have a measure of atrophy, but that is to be expected."

"So what happens next?" Richard didn't want to press the doctor, but he wanted to rejoin Grace. His mother would need relief from her long day as well.

"Next, we schedule another appointment." He closed the folder and regarded Richard with a serious look. "I will perform a handful of more extensive tests, and if those produce the results I expect, we will discuss the details of an operation."

Richard was about to jump up from the chair. He froze at that last word. "Operation?" Just repeating it produced a sinking feeling in his gut. "What kind of operation?"

"There is no need to be concerned. Not at this stage." The doctor's voice held a practiced calm. "We'll know more after Grace's next appointment. And at that time, we will discuss the matter further." He rose, and Richard did the same. "I have a great deal of hope for your niece, Mr. Baxton. You have done an admirable job keeping her limber and making her an excellent candidate to proceed further."

"Doctor, that is music to my ears." Richard glanced over his shoulder toward the door. "Does Grace know? Have you said anything to her?"

The doctor smiled. "Not yet. I wanted to leave the honor to you." He gestured toward the door, silently inviting Richard to precede him.

Richard pushed the door open, revealing an anxious Grace, who sat with her arms braced against the arms of the wheeled chair, almost lifting herself out of it in anticipation.

"Doctor, thank you again." Richard held out his hand, and the doctor gave him a firm handshake. Richard always appreciated such handshakes as well as direct eye contact in all of his business dealings. The doctor didn't disappoint.

The doctor gestured toward the front desk. "If you speak with my assistant, she will see that your next appointment is scheduled, and we can proceed from there."

Richard made quick work of the appointment then joined Grace and his mother.

"What did you find out?" His niece's anxiety was obvious in her voice and facial expression, while Mother looked bemused.

Richard stepped behind Grace's chair and took hold of the handles, silently propelling her toward the main doors.

"You're not going to tell me yet, are you Uncle Richard?"

He smiled as she looked up at him. "Not right now, no. We will have plenty of time to talk in the carriage on the way home." Two attendants held open the double doors for them, and Richard nodded his thanks. "I'm afraid you will simply have to be patient for a bit longer."

She sighed and turned around. "Very well. If you insist."

Richard almost laughed at how stoically Grace sat in her chair. She stared straight ahead and didn't utter a single word until they reached their carriage. The footman greeted them and assisted Mother first before helping Richard get Grace safely tucked inside. Once again, Richard was grateful for the use of his brother's carriages and staff. The affairs of the family business might not be settled, but at least he could continue to make use of his brother's employees and belongings in the interim.

"Are we headed home, sir?" the driver called down from his perch.

"Yes, Jacob, we are."

"Very good, sir."

Richard climbed inside, and the footman closed the door. As soon as the carriage started moving, Grace commenced with the interrogation. She pulled the blanket over her legs up to her waist and twisted her upper torso as best she could to face him.

"So, what did the doctor say? Did he tell you anything different? Why did you smile and seem so pleased when you came out of his office? Why did we have to make another appointment? And is anything in that sack for me?"

Mother sighed and leaned back against the cushioned interior. "I'm certainly happy to know you shall handle this barrage of questions. I believe I'll take advantage of our long ride and rest a spell."

Richard patted his mother's hand. "It's been a long day, and I appreciate your being available to stay with Grace. Now close your eyes and don't give us another thought."

His mother did just that, and Richard focused his attention on his niece. Her last question stuck out. He glanced at the sack from Cobblestone Books, lying on the bench. He should have known she'd see that right away. He couldn't hide it anywhere other than with the driver, but he'd wanted the books with them inside the carriage so he could present them to Grace.

"All right. One question at a time. First, the doctor complimented us on continuing with the exercises every day, and he said it has helped you stay strong despite your paralysis. He was quite impressed with how you responded to the tests he performed, and he wants to see you again so he can conduct a few more tests before deciding if you're able to have surgery."

"Surgery?" Her eyes brightened. "You mean he thinks something can be done to help me? He actually said he can do it?"

"He didn't say he could guarantee anything, but he did say he had a good feeling about it all. He'll know more after your next appointment. We can talk more about it then."

"All right." She placed her hands primly in her lap and smiled. "Now, what is in the sack? Is it for me?"

"As a matter of fact"—he moved the sack to his lap—"there is something in here for you." He peeked inside then gave Grace a teasing grin. "But I am not certain I should show you everything at once. Perhaps just one at a time."

"One at a time is fine with me!" Grace clapped in rapid succession. "I can make the fun last longer that way."

"Very well." Richard reached inside the sack, intentionally making a grand show of retrieving the first book. He nearly laughed at the anxious expression on Grace's face and the way her fingers wiggled, as if they itched to hold the treasure he would soon produce. "This is your first surprise."

"Oh! A new book!" Grace reached across the space between the two seats to take possession of the copy of *Ivanhoe* Richard handed to her. "Sir Walter Scott," she read then looked at her uncle. "So what is this one about?"

Richard breathed a silent prayer of thanks that Miss Pringle had given him a brief sumLaura of each book as she pulled it from the shelves. "That one is about a man named Ivanhoe who comes home from the Crusades and gets caught in the middle of a battle between King Richard, the Lionheart, and his brother, John. But all he really wants to do is claim his inheritance and the woman he loves, Rowena."

"King Richard? That's your name."

He chuckled again. "Well, yes, only I am not a king."

"I bet you could be one if you had to be."

Ah, the unfailing trust of a child. It warmed his heart to see how much his niece loved him. "Thank you for that, Grace. But I think I'll leave the kingdom ruling to those in royalty. I have enough to worry about here without having to think about making decisions for an entire country."

Grace tilted her head and stared at the cover of the book. "I think I agree. I would much rather read about them than live like them." She set the book down and held out a hand for the next. "Can I see the next surprise?"

"Please?"

"Please," she added dutifully.

He reached in and pulled out *Oliver Twist*, hesitating a moment before handing it to her. "Now, this one I only want you reading during the day, and I would like you to read it when I am nearby."

She took the book and looked at the title. "Why? Is it scary?"

"Not so much scary as it contains some parts that could make you very sad, and some people in the story are very cruel. I want you nearby so you can ask questions or talk about the book when you want."

"All right." She shrugged.

Richard hadn't been too sure about that book when Miss Pringle had suggested it. He'd read it himself as a boy, but that was just it. He was a boy. And he didn't mind the fights or the orphanage or the street scenes. Some might say it wasn't proper reading for a young girl, but that had never stopped him before. Besides, his brother and sister-in-law had told him many times about the kinds of books Grace read. She was wise beyond her years, and he was confident she could handle the story.

"I'm going to give you the rest of the books all at once. No sense prolonging the surprise since you already have two of them."

Her eyes widened, and excitement lit up her face. "How many more are there?"

"Three," he replied, "for a total of five." He handed *Nicholas Nickleby*, *The Three Musketeers*, and *Alice's Adventures in*

Wonderland to her and waited for her to read the titles.

"I haven't heard of this Nicholas one, but I know the other two. Mother loved to read—" She fell silent.

Richard leaned forward and touched her hand. "It's all right, Grace. It's only been a few months. Memories of your mother and father and all the good times you shared are sure to make you sad. You miss them a lot. So do I."

She looked up with unshed tears gathering in her eyes. He wanted nothing more than to pull her onto his lap and comfort her. So he moved from his seat and squeezed in between her and the side of the carriage then lifted her into his lap. Several tears fell and moistened his coat, leaving a damp spot where they soaked into the material.

He brushed back her hair from her face and kissed the top of her head. "And now we have another reason for you to have these new books. Every one you read will help you remember your mother and father that much more, and we can discuss those memories together. Miss Pringle assured me you would love all five books, and I have no doubt about that."

"Miss Pringle?" Grace leaned back and looked at him. She wiped at her eyes and sniffled. "You saw Miss Pringle today? So you went to Cobblestone Books for these."

The abrupt change in her demeanor made him press back against the cushion. One minute, she was mourning the loss of her beloved parents, and the next, her eyes were bright with inquisitiveness and a spark of mischief. It felt like night and day.

"Yes. Yes, I did." Richard wiped the tear track on one of her cheeks and smiled. "Your appointment with the specialist was going to take a while, so I decided to make the journey and get you something special after having to endure all that testing."

"What did you say to her? How long were you at the shop? Did she ask about me? About why I wasn't there? Was her sister Anastasia there? When will you be seeing her again?"

He held up his hands. "Whoa! Again the barrage of questions. I can only answer so many." Carefully shifting his position, Richard placed Grace back on the seat and arranged the blanket across her legs. Then he returned to his seat next to his dozing mother so he could see his niece better. She obviously didn't need comforting anymore, so there was no reason for either one of them to be uncomfortable.

A sheepish grin appeared on her lips, and she ducked her head. "I'm sorry, Uncle Richard. But I wish I could have been there. I wish I could have seen you talking to her."

"We'll have to make sure you go next time." Then his mind focused on the last part of her statement. "Wait a moment. Why do you wish you could have seen me talking to her?"

The excitement returned. "When will we be going back?" she asked, ignoring his question.

Richard laughed. "I don't know. I suppose it all depends on how long it takes you to read those books I just purchased for you and when you will need more material to read."

Grace looked down at the books in her lap. "Oh, right. I will get started on them right away." She placed both hands on top of the stack then fixed him with a probing gaze. "So what did the two of you talk about, and how long did you stay?"

If he hadn't known any better, Richard might have thought his niece had turned into a detective or newspaper reporter.

"You answer my question, and I will answer yours. Fair is fair. Why do you wish you could have seen me talking to Miss Pringle?"

"No reason." She looked away. "She seemed so nice, and you were in a better than good mood after meeting her. I spent most of the time with her sister, and I want to know more about Miss Pringle. That's all."

Richard wasn't sure he believed that to be the only reason. Grace didn't generally keep secrets from him. At least not that he noticed. But this time, she seemed to be acting more evasive than normal. Perhaps more would come out if he kept her talking.

"We talked about you, mostly," he said, returning to her list of questions. "When I entered the shop, she looked around and remarked that I appeared to be missing someone."

Grace smiled. "She remembered me."

"Of course she did, you silly goose. You aren't exactly easy to forget."

A self-satisfied smile formed on her lips. "I know."

Richard shook his head. Leave it to an eleven-year-old to be blunt and precocious. But at least he always knew how she felt and usually knew what she was thinking.

"What did you tell her about me?"

"Let's see." He placed his thumb and index finger on either side of his clean-shaven chin. "I told her about your appointment today and the other specialists we've seen. I told her about the accident, everything you told me about it."

"Was she sad, too?"

"Yes. She was sad to hear you had to go through all of that. And sad you lost your parents." He forced a brighter tone to his voice. "But she believes as I do that God has something very special planned for you. We just have to wait and see what He has up His sleeve."

Grace giggled. "God doesn't have sleeves."

"And how do you know? Have you seen Him?"

"Nobody can see Him. He's invisible and everywhere at once. But I know He doesn't have sleeves."

"And you are absolutely certain about that?"

She gave a succinct and determined nod of her head. "Absolutely."

"Well, I'll take your word for it. But I think I'm going to save my opinion until I can see for myself."

"Then I will, too." She again placed her hands in her lap. "Now, what else did you say to Miss Pringle about me?"

"Oh, we are back to that again, are we?" He grinned. "I thought we were done."

"But you didn't get to the best part."

"What best part?"

She crossed her arms. "The part where you talked about the books I like."

"And how do you know we talked about that?"

"Because she picked out these five books"—Grace touched the stack on her lap—"just for me. She wouldn't have known which books to pick if you hadn't told her what I liked."

"How very astute of you."

"I'm smart just like you, Uncle Richard."

"Actually, I think your intelligence comes from your parents." Best to keep his brother's memory alive, along with Grace's mother. He wanted her to be proud of them and of being their daughter.

"But you are my father's brother," she countered with stubborn certainty. "So you could have it, too."

How could he argue with that logic? If she was this smart now, there was no telling what she'd be like as she got older. He might be in for quite the adventure. He only prayed he could keep up with her and give her everything she needed. If it weren't for his mother's assistance, he didn't know how he'd manage. His life and their livelihood remained up in the air until the family business affairs were settled. But he didn't want to think about that now.

"All right. You win." He relaxed against the back of the seat cushion. "Intelligence runs in our family, and we all have it." Richard glanced out the window and took note of their surroundings. "Why don't you start reading one of your books? I'm going to close my eyes for a little rest until we reach home."

"Very well."

If only all instructions and decisions were received and made so easily.

five

Charlotte pulled the needle through the cotton shift she was mending. Good thing the task didn't require much of her attention. She doubted she could muster up much more concentration.

"Ouch!"

"Be careful, Charlotte," Anastasia warned. "That's the third time in the last ten minutes you've stuck yourself with the needle. You're usually more attentive than that."

She was. But lately she had trouble keeping her mind on anything other than her bookshop, Mr. Baxton, and his darling niece. After hearing the story of Grace's accident, Charlotte felt her heart going out to the girl even more.

Three weeks. It had been three weeks since Charlotte had last seen Mr. Baxton. Despite it being foolish, she had begun watching for him after only one week. Common sense told her it had been a little over two weeks between his first and second visits, and this time, she had sent him home with one more book. But try telling that to her heart and the hope it held of seeing him again.

At least Anastasia had been occupied with her special school project. She'd only been at the bookshop one day a week, so Charlotte hadn't had to endure too much teasing when she watched the door for Mr. Baxton's appearance. At home, though, her sister was ruthless. She'd even managed to get their more peaceful sister, Bethany, involved.

"Charlotte? Are you all right?"

A hand on her arm made her stop mid-stitch. "What?" She turned to see Anastasia looking at her with concern.

"I asked if you were all right. Bethany and I have been telling you about the cotillion you missed last weekend. But you were miles away, lost in thought."

Look at what daydreaming of Mr. Baxton did. She had to stop this.

"I'm sorry." She dropped her shoulders and sighed, letting her hands and the shift fall to her lap. "I'm afraid my thoughts have been centered on the bookshop of late."

Bethany glanced up. "Your shop—or on a certain gentleman customer?"

Anastasia giggled. "And his resilient niece." The two younger sisters shared a private look. "Is it any wonder she's managed to put the needle into her thumb more times than through the shift she's mending?"

"This gentleman has our sister rather besotted."

Charlotte sighed. She truly needed this. Straightforward, no-nonsense talk to help her clear her head. . .even if it was delivered courtesy of her scheming younger sisters.

Bethany leveled a suspicious look in her direction. "So is what Anastasia tells me true? You hear the bell above your shop door chime and every time hope it's this Mr. Baxton returning to see you?"

"Yes," she admitted in a whisper.

"I told you so." Anastasia clapped her hands and bounced up and down as much as the wingback chair would allow. "Our dear Charlotte has finally met a man who has captured her attention. And now she wishes to make him her beau."

"I never said I wanted him for a beau," Charlotte protested.

Then again, perhaps her sister was right. She might not know much about Mr. Baxton, but she knew what was important. That he trusted God, cared deeply for his niece, accepted responsibility when it was given to him, and was a man of his word. She could certainly do far worse. But as of right now, their relationship was nothing more than friendship. If she could even call it that.

"You didn't." Anastasia nodded. "But you didn't say you *didn't* want him for a beau either," she added with a smirk. "And with Mother called away to tend to dinner preparations, we have the freedom to pursue this line of questioning."

Charlotte leveled a glare at her younger sister, but the girl wouldn't be dissuaded.

"Come now, Anastasia." Bethany maintained a level tone to her voice. "Let's not take things too far."

Ah good. A voice of reason. At least she had Bethany on her side.

"After all," Bethany continued, turning back toward Charlotte with a gleam in her eyes. "If we're not careful, we might cause our dear Charlotte to become exasperated and despondent. Then we'd never find out the secrets this gentleman possesses that have so enraptured our dear sister as to make her lose her concentration while performing the simple task of sewing."

Charlotte slapped her hands on the arms of her chair. "That is not the way it is, at all, you two. You're turning two minor little exchanges into something of extraordinary proportions."

"But of course!" Anastasia spread her arms wide. "It's what we do best! How else would we manage to extract the necessary information from you if not by extreme measures?"

Charlotte looked at her two sisters. Their faces indicated genuine earnestness. Then the corner of Anastasia's mouth twitched.

"Ah-ha!" Charlotte pointed a finger at each one in turn, mirth bubbling up from inside. "I knew it. You two couldn't fool anyone with that ruse."

Bethany placed one hand on her chest and faked an innocent expression. "Why, whatever do you mean?" The batting of her eyelashes only made it worse.

Charlotte pressed her lips tight to hold back the laughter, and it came out more like a loud snort. That was all it took. The three sisters leaned toward one another as giggles and merriment overtook them.

Bethany recovered first, straightening and taking several deep breaths to regain her composure. Anastasia sat up as well, her arms holding her middle as she gasped for air. Charlotte struggled to catch her own breath. Her sides hadn't hurt that much in months.

"All right. All right." Bethany splayed her hands, palms down, as if attempting to quiet a rowdy group of children. "Let's make an attempt at being civil, shall we?"

Leave it to Bethany to get everything back under control. Always the voice of reason. She led by example as she picked up the pieces of fabric she was stitching to make a skirt. When they all settled back to their respective tasks, Bethany inhaled then released a single breath.

"Now, Charlotte, *dear*. Why don't you finish telling us about this gentleman before our efforts to find out more are waylaid yet again?"

Charlotte could not escape. She crossed her ankles and adjusted her skirts. Looking straight ahead, she delivered the answer she hoped they wanted to hear.

"It's really not as significant as the two of you make it sound." Charlotte rushed to continue. "Yes, I will admit Mr. Baxton and his niece have touched a chord in my heart with little Grace's plight. But I do not wish to make Mr. Baxton my beau," she said with a brief pointed look at Anastasia, who ducked her head. "Right now, considering him a friend might be presumptuous of me. So let's call him a potential faithful customer, all right?"

"And has he asked you to call him by his first name yet?" Bethany asked. "Or are you still using formal address when you greet one another?"

"I only know him as Mr. Baxton." Charlotte placed her palms on her skirt and slid them toward her knees. "As I said, I am not certain he wishes to be a friend, but even if he had made that request of me, I likely would not tell you, lest it provide you with more ammunition for your cross-examination."

Bethany gasped. "We would never take advantage of something such as that!"

"Oh, I would!" Anastasia piped up. "Anything to begin arranging a potential suit between them."

Charlotte shrugged. "I do so hate to disappoint you both, but there truly isn't much more to say." Actually, there was, but disclosing the unspoken mannerisms she'd observed might not be the best thing to do right now.

"When are you going to see him again?" Bethany asked.

"I am not sure. It has been three weeks since he was last in my shop, and he promised he would return." She knew him to be a man of his word, but she wished he had given a more specific time frame.

"Very well." Bethany assumed a nonchalant air. "Since it appears there isn't anything further to extract from you, I suppose we have no choice but to return to our sewing."

Anastasia narrowed her eyes. "Yes." She jutted her chin into the air. "But I'm certain there will be more. We'll discover it all eventually. And when we do. . ." A teasing gleam entered her eyes, and she rubbed her hands together.

"Discover what?" Mother asked as she entered the room to join them in their sewing. "Thank goodness the matter of dinner has been settled," she said as she settled into the chair she'd recently vacated. "Now what have you three girls been discussing in my absence?"

"Oh, just the repeat visit of a certain Mr. Baxton to Charlotte's bookshop," Anastasia replied with a coy smile.

Mother's face showed interest. "So he returned?" She directed her question at Charlotte.

"Yes, but his niece was not with him."

"Did you extend the invitation your father and I discussed?"

Charlotte relayed what she hoped was an apologetic expression to her mother. "No, ma'am. I am sorry. It completely slipped my mind."

"No doubt because something else occupied it," Bethany said under her breath.

Charlotte gave her sister a swift kick, but Bethany anticipated the action and moved her legs out of reach. "I promise, Mother, the next time I see him, I will extend your invitation." That conversation would likely be awkward, so another thought came to mind. "Perhaps to aid my memory, I can give him a letter stating your wishes."

"Yes, that would be most appropriate." Mother nodded. "I shall compose it later this evening and leave it for you to take with you to the shop tomorrow." She began the methodical motion of needlepoint as an amused smile formed on her lips. "I gather from the end of the conversation I interrupted that there is some uncertainty regarding this Mr. Baxton?"

Bethany waved a hand in the air. "Oh, it is merely Charlotte being overly cautious and not willing to admit the possibilities."

Mother gave Charlotte an approving glance before shifting her focus to her middle daughter. "Being cautious is not a negative trait. I applaud it."

"Bethany and Anastasia are merely reading more into the situation than presently exists. As I told them, I am not certain anything further will develop."

"Something will happen," Anastasia stated. "I am sure of it."

"Be that as it may," Mother replied, "it hasn't happened yet. And I believe we owe it to Charlotte to respect her privacy and not meddle any further on the subject."

Charlotte picked up her shift to resume making repairs. Her sisters didn't seem hurt or offended, and for that she was grateful. Still, it wouldn't hurt to reassure them, just in case.

"If that time comes, I promise you'll be the first to know."

"We'd better be!" Anastasia threatened in a non-aggressive manner.

In the meantime, Charlotte prayed she could maintain her focus as well as her professionalism when it came to seeing Mr. Baxton again.

ꝛ

"Mother, you cannot expect me to be in attendance at every one of these social functions." Charlotte looked over the list again. She saw enough events to keep three young women busy, let alone one.

Her mother glanced up from where she stood repositioning flowers in the vase on the table in the front hall. "I expect you to do as you're told, the same as all the other times the cotillion season has come to a close."

"But I'm at the bookshop all day. I have work to do."

"And I don't?" Her mother gestured loosely about the expanse of the manor. "It isn't easy managing a home of this size, along with the household staff we employ."

"I didn't mean that, Mother." Charlotte held up the list. "I meant there simply won't be time for me to come home, dress, and be ready for each of these events. You are already here and can make time in your day to dress."

"Then you will simply have to leave your shop early enough to allow adequate time to prepare." Her mother sighed. "I am not the one who decided to begin a profession when you had a more than ample livelihood provided for you right here at home."

Charlotte had lost count of how many times she'd had this conversation with her mother over the past year and a half. Her father had been the one to provide the funds for her to purchase the shop. He had arranged for his colleagues to donate books so she wouldn't have to buy everything. He had even called in a favor with one of his friends to craft the artistic wooden shingle that hung over the entrance. And all of this he'd done in spite of her mother's censure.

It just wasn't worth it to go down that path again. There was no changing her mother's mind, although just the other day, Mother had seemed to be congenial about the bookshop. Or perhaps she'd been expressing support of the potential Mr. Baxton brought. That would be more in line with Mother's view of things.

"And before you say anything further"—her mother broke into her thoughts—"allow me to remind you that our family has a reputation among our friends and business associates." The matriarch of the Pringle family smoothed her hands down the front of her tailored day dress. "We are expected to make our appearance at these functions."

Charlotte could almost mouth the words verbatim, as often as she'd heard the speech. *Expected to perform.* Just like puppets on a string controlled by a marionette.

With a look that brooked no argument, her mother continued. "Your sisters will also be there, so perhaps with them by your side, the events will be more bearable."

Charlotte could see beyond her mother's facade of being in control and unaffected. The pinched expression, the look of betrayal, and the hint of disappointment that touched her mother's face revealed she likely feared the worst—her eldest daughter becoming a spinster and a blight on the family name. Mother only wanted Charlotte to blend with the other young ladies of her station, but she'd done that for years. Her compliance had been fruitless. Either the young men only saw her for her dowry and impressive inheritance, or they were so boorish she couldn't bear to spend more than five minutes in their presence. Still, she loved her mother and didn't wish to intentionally bring her pain of any kind.

"Very well, Mother." Charlotte made a mental note to plan

for the dizzying merry-go-round of social events soon to be upon them. "I shall post modified hours at the bookshop and make certain I leave with enough time to prepare for any evening engagement."

Her mother brightened and closed the distance between them. Taking Charlotte's hands, she smiled. "I do appreciate your concession, dear. Please know I don't ask this of you as punishment but as opportunity. You simply never know whom you might meet."

Charlotte didn't want to contradict her mother. But if the gentlemen this season were anything like those of the past six, there would be no surprises.

"I know, Mother. And I promise to do my part. I will also try to enjoy myself." She paused for effect. "No matter how dull the evening might be."

Her mother gave a sardonic grin. "I suppose that is all I can ask." She squeezed Charlotte's hands and released them then turned in the direction of the kitchen. "Now if you'll excuse me, I have to discuss this week's meals with the cook."

As her mother walked away, Charlotte watched her, shoulders erect, head held high, and a certainty of who she was and of her purpose. Although Charlotte possessed some of that same confidence in regard to her bookshop, her purpose within the home had yet to be developed. Charlotte had believed by now she'd be married and starting a family. But that obviously wasn't in God's plan. And until He showed her what His plan was, she'd continue with what she was doing.

She only prayed He wouldn't wait too long.

❧

"I cannot believe you would rather be in your dusty old bookshop than here among these fine ladies and gentlemen, dancing, sharing in the merriment, and wearing your finest gown."

Bethany stood in one of the entryways to the grand room where the dancing had already commenced. Her face was flushed from her recent turn about the floor with the latest gentleman on her dance card. Anastasia had been escorted onto the floor almost as many times as Bethany, each of them leaving Charlotte to wait because her dance-card slot had been empty. Why had she bothered selecting the right gown or fashioning her hair in the latest style? It wasn't as if anyone noticed. Even the men she usually went out of her way to avoid seemed otherwise engaged.

"It is not the dancing and the actual event I detest," Charlotte countered. "It's the boorish gentlemen bent on showcasing every reason they might be considered eligible and the money mongers only interested in my dowry and inheritance."

She glanced around, taking in the crowded yet resplendent ballroom, with a gilded, floor-to-ceiling mirror taking up almost all of one long wall. Two crystal chandeliers hung suspended from the ceiling, ablaze with light.

"I can understand that," Bethany said. "After all, it isn't pleasant to be in the company of a gentleman who speaks highly only of himself."

Charlotte nodded and glanced at her sister. "That is exactly how I feel. It's good to know someone shares my feelings." She turned her focus to the room.

The far wall featured two paned windows, just one section shy of reaching the ceiling, and French doors leading out to the marble terrace. Rich burgundy draperies hung at the windows, but they'd been tied back to allow a view of the gardens. Charlotte had been in her fair share of ballrooms, but the Stuyvesants had done a beautiful job with the overall design and craftsmanship of their home. Even the polished hardwood floors gleamed, despite the overabundance of people treading on the surface.

"But if you don't give them a chance," her sister continued, "how will you know if they become more suitable?" Bethany always tried to present the logical side of the situation. She smoothed her right hand down the front of her pale yellow silk and satin gown, her fingers running across the gathered seams at the empire waistline. The color set off her milk chocolate tresses and warm skin tones to perfection. "After all," she continued, fluffing out her skirts, "some men simply aren't adept at conversation upon the initial introduction. Perhaps they need a little time to grow accustomed to you before their true intentions or personalities can be appreciated."

Charlotte had considered that possibility, but she'd also observed many of these men in other situations. From what she could tell, there hadn't been much difference in their behavior.

"I have given a number of them a chance, and they have yet to prove me wrong. It makes it very difficult to believe any differently."

"And an attitude like that might very well keep you unattached and on your way to spinsterhood."

"Bethany! You shouldn't be so merciless." Anastasia curtsied to the young man who had escorted her from the dance floor and turned to face her sisters only once her dance partner was safely out of hearing. "Now what is this about being a spinster?" She tucked her hand into the crook of Charlotte's arm. "Surely you aren't referring to our dear sister, here."

"Yes." Bethany turned to face Charlotte with an apologetic expression. "I am sorry if I sounded callous. That wasn't my intention." She reached out and took Charlotte's free hand. "But you and I both must face the reality that we are not getting any younger. The number of suitable partners is dwindling every day."

Charlotte nodded. "Yes, Mother reminds me of that quite often. How could I possibly forget?"

"Well, you are the eldest daughter." Anastasia squeezed her arm. "It's up to you to set an example for Bethany and me."

Charlotte looked down into the amused face of her youngest sister. "I've attempted to set an example for you both in many other ways, all of which you have disregarded. Why should my engagement, or lack thereof, be any different?"

Anastasia shrugged. "We need to have at least *one* aspect of your life upon which to pattern our own." She cracked an impish grin.

"Thank you very much." Charlotte pressed her lips into a thin line. "I am pleased to hear at least something in my life and character has the possibility of containing a morsel of interest."

Her two sisters immediately leaned close and embraced her from each side.

"Oh Charlotte," Anastasia said. "You know we are only teasing you."

"Yes," Bethany added. "I am certain you have at least two traits to which we aspire." She winked.

"You two are incorrigible!"

Anastasia smiled. "And you wouldn't have it any other way."

Charlotte returned their hugs, placing her arms around each of their waists. "On that point, you are correct. As to the rest, we will have to wait and see." She glanced toward the dance floor where some gentlemen were leading ladies away from the center and others were seeking their next partners. "Now if I'm not mistaken, you both have the next dance claimed on your dance cards."

"And for the one after that, you have the privilege of dancing with Beauregard Parrish." Anastasia covered her mouth with her hand and muted her giggle.

"Now, now. He isn't that bad," Bethany added, fighting hard to maintain her composure. "If you can get past his clumsy feet and sweaty palms."

Two gentlemen approached at that moment, seeking to claim Anastasia and Bethany for the next dance and saving Charlotte from having to respond. She shook her head. She might not have a full dance card, but her sisters' merriment—and especially Anastasia's escapades—more than made up for it. She could simply live vicariously through them.

If only the gentlemen she encountered could be half as good at conversation as Mr. Baxton, she might actually enjoy the time she spent with them. But for now, she had no choice but to be polite and represent her family well. In the back of her mind, though, she'd count the days until Mr. Baxton's return.

six

"Now, make these windows sparkle and shine, Zachariah, and I might be able to find another nickel or two for you." Charlotte tousled the boy's hair and winked.

"Yes, ma'am, Miss Charlotte!" The lad gave her a quick salute, his uncombed, light brown hair falling across his forehead and nearly covering his eyes. He grabbed his bucket of sudsy water and went straight to work.

Charlotte reached for the handle on the door just as another hand grasped it.

"Allow me," the now familiar, velvety timbred voice offered.

Her cheeks warmed, and Charlotte nodded to Mr. Baxton as he held the door for her. "Thank you," she said, preceding him into the bookshop and silently chastising herself for her telltale reaction to seeing him again.

Mr. Baxton didn't seem to notice. Instead, he removed his hat and held it loosely at his side; then he turned back toward the front of the shop. As he glanced out the windows, she took note of his beaver hat with the fine fabric lining and leather hatband. It sported a bound edge sewn on the brim. From his clothing and mannerisms, she already suspected he didn't come from the working class and could well be a member of the family her parents knew. The high quality of his hat served to confirm her assessment.

"Does that young lad work for you often?" Mr. Baxton turned and gestured with his head toward Zachariah meticulously scrubbing at the front windows.

Charlotte tapped a finger to her lips. "It's been several

months, now. Of course he doesn't come around much during the winter."

"He appears to be quite thorough."

"Yes, he does excellent work." Charlotte took two steps closer to Mr. Baxton and peered out the window. She didn't want Zachariah to see her watching him, so she straightened an already tidy display. "He first approached me last summer, offering to wash my windows and complete any other tasks I might have."

"Does he live nearby?"

Charlotte couldn't determine why Mr. Baxton showed such interest in the lad. "Actually, he lives down by Brandywine Creek, but he spends a great deal of time in and around the park." She picked up two books and held them against her chest. "From what he has told me, he comes here to look for work because there isn't much opportunity where he lives."

Mr. Baxton turned to face her, compassion in his eyes. "It appears you hired well. I am certain some of my household staff would love to have a lad like him around to help with odd jobs." A quick glance over his shoulder preceded a brief sigh. "Pity he doesn't live closer to Ashbourne Hills."

Charlotte chuckled. "You might tell him that before he leaves. It's sure to give him a great deal of pleasure coming from a gentleman such as yourself."

Mr. Baxton gave a succinct nod. "I believe I shall." He turned to fully face her, merriment dancing in eyes the color of caramel. "Now, before we proceed any further with our conversation, Miss Pringle, allow me to apologize for not bestowing a greeting upon my arrival. I must confess I overheard your instructions to the lad and saw how he set right to work, and it distracted me."

"That is quite all right, Mr. Baxton. But to reassure you, your apology is accepted."

He gave a slight bow. "Thank you very much."

Instead of stepping behind the counter, Charlotte remained at the end of it. Far too often, she felt the counter placed a barrier between her and her customers. Sometimes she needed that distance. But at times like this one, the obstruction hindered the conversation.

"Has Grace finished the books I sent home with you last, and might you be here for more?"

"Yes." He followed her to the counter. "And once again, I must praise you for your excellent selections. I had a great deal of difficulty pulling Grace away from those books to see to her studies."

She placed one hand over her chest. "Oh, I am truly sorry."

He brushed off her apology with a wave of his hand, his gaze direct. "I didn't say that to cause contrition on your part; rather, I meant to demonstrate how much she enjoyed reading those stories." He snapped his fingers. "Ah yes, and *Oliver Twist.* She had the most questions about that one, but I did as you suggested and only allowed her to read it when she was in my presence. It worked out rather well. She read parts of it aloud." A smile formed on his lips. "Brought back memories of when I read it as a boy."

"I am pleased to hear she handled it well. Some younger readers become quite affected when they read it. Either they are frightened by the characters of Fagin and Bill Sykes, or they are overcome with remorse about the situations. Mr. Dickens went into great detail in that dark tale."

As if life for some children didn't already come with its fair share of challenges. To read such a grim story and to see the corrupt institutions in England depicted in such a vile manner would make even the most stalwart reader experience a strong pang of conscience.

Mr. Baxton allowed a half grin and placed his free hand in his pocket. "Well, perhaps the next collection of books I bring her will not contain any brooding stories."

"I shall endeavor to make certain of that."

The bell above the door jingled, and Charlotte looked up to see an acquaintance of hers enter. Amelia Devonshire had been a self-named friend for many years, but she also spent most of her time seeking out gossip-worthy details to share with everyone she knew. Most of the time, she did so without malicious intent. A few times, however, the gossip had turned sour, and the object of Amelia's tales had suffered greatly.

"Good afternoon, my dear Charlotte." Amelia swept into the shop like a feather on a cloud, full of grace and effortless elegance.

"Good afternoon, Amelia. How nice of you to come for a visit."

Charlotte cast a quick glance at Mr. Baxton, grateful his back was to Amelia. He narrowed his eyes slightly and seemed to pick up on something she conveyed. Had she visibly reacted to Amelia's appearance? If so, she hoped Amelia hadn't seen it, too. Regardless, Mr. Baxton stepped away from the counter, allowing Amelia the chance to approach.

"Miss Pringle, thank you again for your suggestion," he said. "I believe I shall spend a little time browsing before making my final decision." With a nod, he disappeared down the aisle that housed books similar to the ones he'd purchased earlier.

"Should you have any questions, please do not hesitate to ask," she called to his retreating back.

"Well, it isn't often I have the opportunity to visit while you actually have a customer." Amelia stepped closer. Taking Charlotte's hands in hers, she gave them a light squeeze and smiled. "It appears most of what I have been hearing about your increased patronage of late is true. How have you been, dear?"

❧

Richard stayed close to the front, peeking around the books

in order to observe Miss Pringle interacting with the other young woman. They kept their voices low, but he could read Miss Pringle's facial expressions. The conversation made her both wary and uncomfortable. He didn't dare move closer and risk revealing his attempt at eavesdropping. He shouldn't be doing it anyway. But something about Miss Pringle's mannerisms compelled him to keep watch. The other young lady likely didn't intend any harm, but Richard still felt protective.

"Is the gentleman in question present in your shop this very moment?"

Uh-oh! Richard hadn't heard Miss Pringle's response or even the comment that led to the woman's question. But since he was the object of their conversation, he should appear preoccupied. Unfortunately, Richard couldn't determine what these books in front of him had in common. Since he *should* be browsing through the books suitable for Grace, he would have no choice but to confess his guilt were someone to ask.

Richard developed an odd sense that someone watched him as he stood in the aisle, staring at the shelves. From the corner of his eye, he cast a look to his left and caught sight of the young woman Miss Pringle addressed as Amelia. The lady—if one could call her that—unabashedly stared at him and made no attempt to hide her lack of discretion. He did his best to remain still, appearing as unaffected as he could manage, until she disappeared from view.

A few moments later, Charlotte's visitor turned toward the door, but not before casting a final glance in his direction. The young woman departed, leaving him alone again with Miss Pringle. A moment or two later, another customer entered, but he went straight to a specific section of books without a word to anyone.

Richard waited several more minutes before locating the section where he'd find books for Grace. After pulling two from the shelf, he made his way to the front of the shop. Miss Pringle looked up when he approached, then quickly averted her gaze, busying herself with straightening an already immaculate area around the cash register. He had seen only one other such register during his time spent along the Ohio River. It had been invented in Dayton, and he had spoken to James Ritty in Cincinnati about the inspiration behind the creation. He'd have to ask Miss Pringle how she came to acquire one, but not now. She glanced over his shoulder toward the back of the shop, no doubt looking after her most recent customer.

"I believe I've found two more books Grace will enjoy," he said without preamble.

Miss Pringle turned to face him, fully composed. "Wonderful." Her smile seemed genuine, but a hint of wariness lay just behind it. She took the books from him and looked at the titles. "Ah yes. *Little Women* and *The Adventures of Tom Sawyer*." She totaled them on the register, and he handed her the cash. "Both excellent choices," she said as the drawer popped open with a loud bell. She placed his money inside then handed him his change. "They will give her several hours of entertainment."

"Yes. I wanted to give her a little easy reading after the last set." He narrowed his eyes slightly and studied her face. "Forgive me for being presumptuous, Miss Pringle, but is everything all right? You do not seem quite yourself today." Richard jerked a thumb toward the door. "I hope your last visitor didn't upset you."

"No, no. Amelia can be rather trying, but speaking with her didn't affect me adversely." She glanced down at her hands, as if trying to decide whether to share anything with him.

Richard held up a hand. "If you do not wish to speak of it, I understand. As I said, I don't wish to pry."

A soft smile formed on her lips. "Thank you. I appreciate

your concern. Since you did ask, however. . ." She paused then sighed. "I am rather troubled over my mother and the many social engagements she has arranged for me to attend this season. She seems to have no interest in my responsibilities here at the shop. Instead, she tells me repeatedly that I must see to my duty as the eldest daughter and attend because it's expected of me."

"And I am certain you have spoken with her about this." He might not know Miss Pringle well, but certain aspects of her character shone clear and bright. She didn't strike him as a young woman who would avoid speaking her mind when the situation called for it.

Sadness overtook her features. "Yes, but every time we speak of it, the result is the same."

"Let me guess. She would prefer you remain home and attend these social affairs rather than be involved with this bookshop at all."

"Yes, that is it exactly." She brightened somewhat. "My father is responsible for securing this location and assisting me with the loan, as well as collecting books initially so I could open with inventory. My mother didn't want any part of it."

Richard nodded. "And now she feels the bookshop is interfering with you being present as her oldest daughter at these events."

"I'm afraid that is true."

He placed a hand lightly over her fingers, and she startled but didn't pull away. It was a bold move, but he felt the situation warranted it. After waiting for her to make eye contact, Richard softened his expression and allowed the corners of his mouth to turn upward.

"This might not be much consolation, but my older sister endured a similar situation with our mother. Laura didn't care much for the social affairs. She preferred to spend her time reading and studying mathematics. But after much coaxing, she heeded our mother's wishes and met the man she eventually married. Now she lives with him in Ohio, where together, they own a general store." He chuckled. "And she manages their accounting books."

"If only it were that simple. The only thing my mother wants is to see me suitably matched. My happiness doesn't seem to be of any concern to her."

Richard gave her hand a slight squeeze. "Don't give up, Miss Pringle. It might not seem possible right now, but circumstances can change rather quickly. Before you know it, you, too, could find happiness *and* a match that pleases your mother."

"I truly hope it happens that way."

If only he were in a position to be more than a friend. But not yet. He had a few business matters to settle first. An idea struck him. He removed his hand and snapped his fingers then pointed in her direction.

"I know exactly what you need. And it would be perfect for Grace as well."

Her brow knitted in confusion, and for the briefest of seconds, she glanced down at her hand, as if missing the physical contact. He thought he imagined it, but when she looked at him again, he saw a spark in her eyes.

"And what is that, Mr. Baxton?"

"First, I would like to invite you to join Grace and me on a picnic in the park the next time we visit. My cook will provide all the food." He gave her what he hoped was an inviting look paired with a hint of playfulness. "You only need to bring yourself and your smile."

It worked.

The smile absent from her face since Miss Amelia first came through the door returned. "I should like that very much. Thank you." A twinkle entered her eyes. "And second?"

Second? He blinked a few times to clear his head. Why had he allowed himself to be distracted by her smile and the softness in her features?

"Second. Yes. I would like you to call me Richard." He held up a hand and stayed her potential protest. "You have become an important part of Grace's life. . .and mine. And I feel situations like ours allow for less formality."

She nodded. "Very well. But only if you will also call me Charlotte."

Richard almost took a step back at her easy agreement. He thought for sure he'd have to persuade with more than that one argument. Perhaps she had been thinking along the same lines, but propriety prevented her from saying anything.

"Consider it done." He reached out and raised her fingers to his lips. "Until next time, Miss Charlotte Pringle," he said with a wink. "I shall return in two weeks' time."

"I look forward to it and to seeing Grace, as well."

He released her hand, took his two books, replaced his hat, and turned to leave. At the front door, he tipped the edge of his hat in her direction, maintaining eye contact until the door closed between them. With her blush-tinged face indelibly printed on his mind, he knew the next two weeks would be the longest yet.

seven

"Are we almost there, Uncle Richard?" Grace's pleading made Richard smile. "How much longer?"

Richard looked out the carriage window and saw one of the mills along the Brandywine. "I would estimate about five more minutes." He raised one eyebrow. "Are you certain you can manage patience for that long?"

"I cannot guarantee it, but I shall try."

Honest to a fault. He always knew where he stood with her or what she was feeling. Some might consider that to be brazen in a young girl of her age, but Richard found it refreshing and endearing. It only made him love her that much more. Oh, what his brother was missing. Why had God chosen to take those two lives now? Just when Grace needed them most.

"I can see the river. We're almost there!" Grace clapped in rapid succession, her eyes fixed on the window opposite her.

Good. He could let Grace watch for the bookshop. He needed to plan a little on what he would say to Miss Pringle— that is, Charlotte—once they arrived. Her given name didn't yet come easily to his mind or his lips. He'd been working on it every day since their last meeting. It had nothing to do with the familiarity he'd requested. That he wanted more than anything. But he still battled with whether he overstepped the bounds of propriety in making the request. And he left so soon after. Was Charlotte regretting her agreement? Did she think him ill-mannered or disrespectful? He certainly hoped not.

"Uncle Richard! We're here!"

Grace didn't exactly have to announce their arrival. Richard heard the *clip-clop* of the horse's hooves on the cobblestone street, the noise of the barking dogs in the park, and the echo of voices carried on the wind. Their carriage stopped, and a moment later, the footman opened the door to help them out. Richard lifted Grace against his chest, and she draped her arms around his neck. As he bent through the opening, the footman reached up to take Grace from him. Once she was situated in her chair, Richard turned to retrieve the picnic basket from the boot of the carriage.

"Feel free to move the carriage to a quieter spot along the park," he told the footman. "We will be there for at least an hour, perhaps a little more."

"Very good, sir." The man tipped his hat, and the driver did the same. A moment later, they headed up the street then turned the corner and pulled the carriage to a stop under the shade of a few maple trees.

The setting was so picturesque. He could hardly wait to walk with Charlotte along the path and sit with her as they shared lunch. They wouldn't be alone, but it was close enough for now.

"Can we go to the bookshop?"

Richard glanced down to see Grace looking up at him. No, he and Charlotte wouldn't be alone. Perhaps that was a good thing. With Grace present, there'd be no chance for any other possible proprieties to be trampled.

"Yes Grace. We're going."

After looking up and down the street, Richard hooked the basket on one handle and maneuvered Grace off the sidewalk and across the bumpy cobblestones. Once they made it to the sidewalk on the other side, Richard immediately looked in the direction of the bookshop.

There she was.

Charlotte stood outside, leaning against one of the windows to her shop, her eyes closed and her face upturned. She looked so peaceful. He hadn't expected to find her here, and all the words he'd rehearsed vanished, leaving him unprepared to greet her. But he had to say something, especially before she opened her eyes and saw them.

"Good morning, Miss Pringle." Grace took care of the introduction for him.

"Oh!" Charlotte straightened and pushed off the wall. Her hand went to her chest. "Grace. You startled me."

"I'm sorry, Miss Pringle. I didn't mean to scare you."

She chuckled. "No, no, dear. It's quite all right." Charlotte stepped forward and bent to brush a hand across Grace's cheek. "You didn't frighten me. Startled means surprised more than scared. . .at least in this instance."

"I'm glad to hear that."

Richard smiled. Charlotte appeared more relaxed today. It showed in the smooth lines of her cheeks, the absence of strain in her eyes, and the soft way her mouth curved up when she spoke to Grace.

"You are earlier than I expected." She directed this statement more at him than Grace. "I thought you wouldn't be here until Thursday."

Richard felt the odd urge to stub his toe against the ground and duck his head. Just like when he'd been caught stuffing firecrackers in the stove at school as a young boy. Instead, he met her questioning gaze and offered an apologetic smile.

"Yes. But Grace was so excited to come see you again, and we had today free, so we decided to come."

"That's not true, Uncle Richard," Grace said. "You asked if I wanted to come today because you couldn't focus on your work."

Amusement danced across Charlotte's face. Richard shrugged and held out his hands in a hopeless gesture. What else could he do?

"I suppose it's a good thing I decided not to bring my lunch with me today." Charlotte glanced at the picnic basket hanging from Grace's chair. "I see you came prepared despite the change of days. So now that you are both here, shall we proceed as originally planned?"

"Do you not have to close your shop?"

"No. I haven't had a customer in the past thirty minutes, and this is usually when I take time to have lunch, so there shouldn't be anyone coming until later this afternoon."

Richard nodded. "Very well, then. I believe we'll allow Grace to lead the way."

The three of them crossed the street and headed straight for the park. Grace chattered away as Richard pushed her chair, but her voice and words became nothing but noise with each step they took. His attention remained on Charlotte.

The way she'd swept up her hair gave her a more feminine appearance overall. Not that she lacked femininity in any way. Her gown hugged her trim form nicely, and the rosy shade complemented her complexion. Richard mentally compared her to some of the women he encountered at social engagements back home and in Philadelphia. He sometimes spent more time there than at the shipyards in Wilmington. But those women were besotted with their appearance, and he was grateful Charlotte didn't seem obsessed with having the tiniest waist or the gown with the most frills. No, she had substance to her yet remained trim and healthy.

A second later, Charlotte turned and caught him staring. He quickly averted his gaze and looked straight ahead. From the corner of his eye, he caught her slow grin, but he held the answering one back from his own lips.

"I like this spot. Right here," Grace announced. "Let's set up our picnic on the grass under the tall oak."

Richard glanced at Charlotte. "Will that meet with your approval?"

"Of course," she replied, not really looking at him. She stepped in front of Grace so that the girl could see her. "Grace, you picked a beautiful location."

His niece beamed at the praise. Charlotte was right. The place was perfect. Just enough shade, not a lot of passersby on this particular path, and near enough to the creek to hear the water rushing over the rocks.

In no time, they had the checkered blanket spread on the ground and the food set out for lunch.

"What an amazing meal your cook has prepared!"

"Yes," Richard replied, "she does tend to overdo it, or outdo herself, whichever the case may be."

"I smelled that fried chicken the entire carriage ride and all the while the basket hung on the back of my chair." Grace pouted, looking much younger than her eleven years. "Can we please eat now?"

"Of course." Richard gestured for Charlotte to take a seat, and he lowered himself on the other side of his niece. "Would you like to bless the food, Grace?"

"Yes." The girl bowed her head and closed her eyes, folding her hands in her lap. "Dear Jesus, thank You for the beautiful day You gave us and for the delicious food our cook has made for us to enjoy. I'm especially grateful for Miss Pringle joining us for lunch and a walk in the park. Please help us to have fun and for Uncle Richard to behave himself. Amen."

Charlotte giggled and remained with her head bowed.

"Just what was that all about, young lady?" Richard tried to sound firm, but the innocent expression on his niece's face made it impossible.

"Sometimes you make jokes, and other people don't understand them. Or you try too hard to get people to like you. Miss Pringle already does, or she wouldn't be here with us today. And you know I love you." She shrugged. "So I prayed for Jesus to help you be yourself."

Spoken from the mouth of a babe, just as Scripture stated in the book of Matthew. He should listen more to his niece. It might help him avoid embarrassment. Of course in this case, it only made the embarrassment worse.

"So shall we eat?" he asked, holding up the plate of fried chicken to Charlotte. It was easier to move things along than dig himself a deeper hole.

Charlotte had her lips pressed in a thin line, no doubt attempting to hold back the mirth caused by Grace's prayer. It didn't bother Richard. His niece meant no harm, and he'd rather let Charlotte see the real him than some fake version with the real self buried several layers deep. She seemed to appreciate it and find enjoyment in it as well. And that set the tone for their meal rather nicely.

"Tell me, Grace," Charlotte said once they had served themselves food. "You have read ten or eleven books from my shop. Which one was your favorite, and why?"

Richard had discussed this topic with Grace many times, so he mentally removed himself from the conversation and once again observed Charlotte. She seemed so at ease with Grace. Their interaction was effortless and natural. He was pleased to see his niece warm up to Charlotte so easily. Then again, Grace warmed easily to folks, and almost everyone had trouble resisting her infectious personality.

Propping himself on his left side, Richard enjoyed watching the two interact as he ate his lunch. Every once in a while, Charlotte stole a glance in his direction, and he smiled in return. But for the most part, she remained focused on Grace, giving the girl her undivided attention. And Grace relished it. She needed a younger female influence in her life again. Richard wouldn't mind at all if that person was Charlotte. He had to get these two together more often.

❧

Charlotte kept her legs tucked beneath her and relaxed her

pose as she looked up at Grace. The way the tall oak formed a canopy above them lent a sense of privacy to their little lunch. She wished she owned one of those cameras she'd seen a few times. It could capture this moment and preserve it forever as a photograph. But all those chemicals, and the fragile glass plates. Not to mention lugging the various parts of the contraption around. It was likely more trouble than it was worth. She'd just have to stick with preserving the memory in her mind.

She smiled at Grace. "So *Little Women* is your favorite?"

"I just finished that one on the way to and from my last visit to the doctor." Grace ate her last bite of lemon meringue pie, wiped her mouth, and folded her napkin in her lap, placing her hands on top.

"Was that appointment any better than the others?" Charlotte loved discussing books with Grace, but she also wanted to hear about the chances of the young girl walking again.

Grace looked at her uncle, who nodded. Some unspoken communication took place between them, an understanding to which Charlotte wasn't privy. Again, she marveled at the closeness the two obviously shared. Their relationship prior to the accident must have been special for that bond to have solidified so quickly. She'd met others in similar circumstances, and sometimes the ones thrown together never fully developed an intimate relationship.

"Well, the one before this one was. We heard something new that time," Grace began with hesitation.

"And what was that?" Charlotte asked. "Good news, I hope."

"We aren't sure," the girl said with a tinge of dejection. "The doctor said he thinks there is a chance for me to walk again. And he repeated that at this appointment, too."

Praise God!

"That is wonderful!" she said aloud. But Grace didn't

appear to share her enthusiasm. "Why do you not seem to be happy about hearing this?"

Again Grace looked to her uncle before answering. "Because I have to have an operation, and it's very expensive."

That shouldn't be a problem. From his tailored clothing, to his personal carriage complete with a driver and footman, down to his mannerisms and speech, Richard had demonstrated signs that money was not an issue. And he had to have substantial funds to be able to keep taking Grace to these special doctors so often. Unless of course, the money came from a trust fund for Grace, dispensed following the death of her parents. Still, if she had that, surely they could use those resources to cover the operation. From the looks on both their faces, though, that didn't seem to be an option. Charlotte wanted to learn more, but she wouldn't be discourteous by asking.

"Yes, from what I have heard, operations do cost a great deal of money."

Richard leaned forward to lend his input to the conversation. "The profits from our family's shipping business have been tied up in the transfer of ownership. I have been working on the details every day amidst overseeing the day-to-day running of the business. But some legal issues and personal concerns are causing several problems." He ran his hand across his face. "I am trying to solve them, but each day that passes is one more day from the accident."

He didn't have to say more. With each passing day, the chances grew slimmer for a successful operation. Something like that shouldn't be stated in front of Grace, but the girl had likely figured it out on her own. The hope in her eyes had dimmed almost immediately after mentioning the operation. And the anguish on Richard's face only made the situation more hopeless. Compassion filled Charlotte.

She wished she could do something. But what? Any extra

money she had went right back into the bookshop, paying the rent or restocking books. She didn't have much left over, let alone enough to help with an expensive operation. And she certainly couldn't ask her father for help. He'd already established a dowry along with her inheritance, but both of those were off limits until she married.

"Isn't there a way for you to pay for the operation in smaller amounts over time?" Charlotte ran through possible scenarios in her mind. "I would think it prudent for the hospital and doctor to work with you. At least that way, they would know the money is coming."

Richard nodded. "We did discuss that with the doctor, but their policy is payment in full at the time of services rendered." He massaged an area just above his eyes. "So we departed with the promise we would look into the matter and get back to him as soon as possible."

"And this doctor is your only option? No other doctors perform this operation who might have a different payment policy?" They no doubt had gone through all the options, but Charlotte refused to believe the situation was this hopeless.

"The only other doctors who have ever had success with this procedure live in Chicago, New York, and St. Louis." Richard's mouth drooped into a frown. "At this critical juncture with the family business, we simply cannot afford to make a journey of that distance. And even if we did, we have no guarantee their policy would be any different."

"That's why we have to wait," Grace said.

Her quiet yet despondent tone sounded like all her hope had shattered. Charlotte longed to put a smile back on the girl's face, but how? It was her fault she'd led them down this path in their conversation. The picnic had been going so well up to that point. They'd laughed, talked about books, shared a delicious meal, and enjoyed each other's company. She had to make things right.

"Look on the bright side," Charlotte began. "At least while you wait, you can enjoy the fun of a wheeled chair to help you get around. I must confess, many days I wish *I* could ride in one. . .especially down a hill. It would be almost like sledding, only not as cold."

A little squeak of a giggle escaped Grace's lips, and her eyes showed a faint glimmer of brightness. Charlotte smiled, hoping they were on their way toward more lighthearted topics. She wouldn't forget about their need for funds, but right now, she wanted to enjoy the time they shared.

"Actually, Grace has already experienced the fun of a hill not too far from where we live." A sheepish grin showed on Richard's face. "Of course, that little ride wasn't intentional."

Grace covered her mouth with one hand and laughed. "No, but it was fun." She cast a loving and forgiving glance at her uncle. "And it wasn't your fault you forgot to stop the wheels."

"You're right." Richard offered a crooked grin. "I was still getting used to helping you get around. Everything was all so new to us both."

Good. She'd managed to help them get back to more pleasant memories and conversation. "I gather this experience was both memorable and beneficial to future travels."

"Yes, I have been overly careful ever since."

"Even when I *wanted* to go for a ride," Grace added.

Richard reached for their plates and started to pack them away in the basket.

"Here," Charlotte offered, "let me see to that."

She reached for a plate at the same time, and their hands touched, two of his fingers covering hers. Charlotte froze and stared at the plate. Richard froze, too, but when she looked up, his gaze was fastened on her, not the plate. She tried to break the hypnotic effect of his warm brown eyes, but it was no use.

"If you two don't move faster, we might have to eat what's left for dinner."

Grace's voice broke the spell, and Richard released the plate. A roguish grin formed on his lips as he handed Charlotte the other plates. He helped her gather the remaining food, and in just a few minutes, they had the meal put away. Once Richard hooked the basket on the back of Grace's chair, it made the reality of the end of their time together come crashing in like a wave on the sand. Now would be a good time to extend her thanks.

Charlotte stood and brushed off the loose grass blades from her skirts, sending the dirt to the ground as well. She bent to retrieve her straw hat, set it on her head, and tied the wide ribbon beneath her chin.

"As much as I have enjoyed our time together, I do have to return to the bookshop." Charlotte looked at Grace and Richard. "But I hope to see you both again very soon."

"Oh!" Grace sat up in her chair. "I almost forgot." She withdrew an envelope from a little pocket sewn into her dress. After handing it to Charlotte, she continued. "I would like you to come to my birthday party next month. That invitation"— she nodded at the envelope Charlotte now held—"has all the details. Please say you'll come. And Anastasia is welcome, too."

Charlotte turned the envelope over in her hand. She hadn't expected this. Grace must consider her someone special to invite her to such a personal event. She looked first at Grace then to Richard. His eyes showed his desire for her to join them. How could she turn either one of them down?

"I would be both pleased and honored to accept. Thank you, Grace."

The girl clapped and grinned like the Cheshire Cat in that book by Lewis Carroll.

"It appears to be settled." Richard placed both hands on the handles of Grace's chair. "I'll be sure to send a carriage for you on the day of the party. I'm not certain we'll be seeing you again before then, as Grace has a substantial amount of work to complete to wrap up her studies for this year." He looked down at her just as Grace tipped her head to look up at him.

"He made me promise to finish it all before the party, or he'd tell everyone the party was canceled." Her adorable pout gave her a pixie-like appearance.

Charlotte pressed her mouth into a thin line to avoid laughing. Grace looked so serious.

"Well, I suppose you'd better head straight home so you can get started. We certainly don't want a party to be canceled. They are far too much fun." Charlotte stepped forward until she was nearly toe to toe with Grace. She tipped up the girl's chin with her forefinger and smiled. "And if I know you, you'll have everything completed long beforehand. You'll probably have time left over where you will be twiddling your thumbs, looking for something else to do as you wait."

The pout transformed into a smile, and Grace's entire demeanor changed.

She tapped the arms of her chair. "Let's go, Uncle Richard. I want to get started on my studies."

Richard mouthed a thank-you to Charlotte over Grace's head. Charlotte nodded. Anything she could do to help.

"Shall we make our way back to the shop?" Richard invited.

Charlotte nodded. "I believe we shall."

The trio walked along in silence. Only the thumping of the wheels on Grace's chair against the cobblestone interrupted the stillness. When they reached the front of her shop, Charlotte turned to thank Richard, but the words died in her throat. He looked like he was about to say something. Instead, he stood and shifted from one foot to the other, alternating between licking his lips and looking down at Grace then back up at Charlotte.

Was he going to say anything or not? She didn't know. The awkward silence seemed to stretch for several minutes, when in reality it was only a few moments. This was ridiculous. She had to say something.

"Thank you again for a truly delightful picnic. I very much enjoyed our afternoon together and look forward to coming to your birthday party, Grace." Charlotte winked. "And I am certain Anastasia will be excited to come, as well." She turned partway toward her shop then included both Richard and Grace in her parting words. "As much as I wish I didn't have to leave such charming company, work inside needs my immediate attention. So, I must say good-bye."

Whatever Richard might have eventually said never happened. He did sigh though. Perhaps in frustration at being unable to vocalize his thoughts. Charlotte would likely never know.

"Good-bye, Miss Pringle," Grace called as Richard steered them toward the path.

"Good-bye, Grace. Good-bye, Mr. Ba—I mean Richard."

He grinned and dipped his head. "Have a nice afternoon, Charlotte. Thank you again for joining us."

Charlotte opened the door and headed into her shop. As she shut the door, she looked out the window. After spotting Richard and Grace across the street, she started to turn away but caught Richard pivoting Grace's chair toward the shop. An enthusiastic wave from the young girl accompanied a reserved but meaningful wave from Richard. She returned the wave and finally began her work.

The next month couldn't pass by fast enough.

eight

The entire experience felt like an exercise in futility. Charlotte didn't know why she bothered attending so many of these events, other than obedience to her mother's wishes. At twenty, she should be able to make her own decisions. Yet here she stood, feeling more like wall décor than an invited attendee at the soiree. This made the fifth event this month, and while it helped time pass more quickly, it didn't make her evenings any more enjoyable.

At least the orchestra was playing some of her favorite pieces. Between turns about the floor with her scarce dance card signers, she could listen to the soothing strains of the music.

"So is it just me, or do these events become more intolerable each passing year?"

Charlotte startled at the familiar voice of Margaret Howard, an old schoolmate who'd also suffered through six seasons of social affairs with no success.

"It isn't just you," Charlotte replied. "But I must say it's nice to see someone else who abhors the repetitive carousel of introductions and attempted pairings that accompany these events."

"Oh, I more than abhor them. I no longer attend them for those reasons." Margaret waved her left hand in the air like royalty waving to her subjects. "Now it's become a social expectation."

Charlotte gasped. "Is that what I think it is? Are you wearing an engagement ring and a wedding band?" She took hold of Margaret's hand and inspected the rings. *Stunning*. It was the only word that came to mind, but it fit. She looked up at the twinkling eyes of her friend. "When did this all occur, and how did I miss it? And your last name obviously isn't Howard anymore. So how do I address you?"

Margaret placed her hand in the crook of Charlotte's elbow and leaned in close. "Come with me, and I shall share the entire story."

Her friend led her toward the double doors opposite them, and the two young women stepped out onto the veranda. Charlotte could hardly wait to hear what had happened.

"Are you going to share your fascinating story now?"

Margaret narrowed her gaze and crossed her arms. "Who told you it was fascinating?"

"Any story where you conclude one season without any offers and appear at the next with a ring on your hand must be fascinating." Charlotte raised one eyebrow and grinned. "Do you deny it?"

The young woman laughed. "No. How could I?" She gestured toward the waist-high wall at the edge of the veranda. "Come, let's stand over there. It affords a much better view."

Charlotte regarded her friend carefully. First, she didn't want to talk inside. Now she wanted to share her story but in a specific place on the veranda. Just what was Margaret going to tell her? And why all the secrecy? Not that Charlotte minded, of course. This was the first thing to pique her interest at one of these events all season.

"All right." Charlotte rested her left forearm on the cool stone wall and draped her right hand over her wrist. "We are here. Now tell me before I perish from anticipation." A bit dramatic, yes, but she felt like having a little fun.

"Well. . ." Margaret drew out the word with a grin. "I suppose I should start by saying it all happened unexpectedly. It isn't merely the occurrence of the engagement as much as who made the offer for my hand."

"You already have me intrigued. I should like to learn the identity of this mysterious gentleman before the evening comes to a close and the clock chimes twelve times."

Her friend cast her a glance, one corner of her mouth turning upward in an impish grin. "You always were rather theatrical. Perhaps I should lengthen the anticipation by starting at the beginning and withhold his identity a while longer."

Charlotte faced the gardens below them. White lights illuminated the flower beds and finely trimmed hedges. Even the fountains had been illuminated. It would be the perfect setting to walk with a suitor or potential intended. But since Charlotte didn't have such a man, she could enjoy her friend's story and pretend it was hers.

She shrugged, acting as if it didn't matter either way. She wanted to tease Margaret as much as her friend taunted her. "If you do that, I shall simply walk away and learn the tale from someone else."

Margaret folded her arms. "And just who would you find to divulge every detail to you?"

"I am certain I could find someone."

"Yes, but would they be able to point out the gentleman in question as easily as I?" She extended one long, graceful arm out over the wall toward the gardens.

Charlotte's gaze followed her friend's movement. She peered into the evening twilight. How did Margaret expect her to locate the man among the myriad of people out there? It wasn't as if he wore a shingle advertising his identity. And he likely wouldn't be dressed any differently—

Charlotte blinked several times as her gaze landed on a certain gentleman surrounded by a handful of others as if he were holding court. She recalled the way Margaret had waved her hand to show off her rings. No. That couldn't be the man she meant. Charlotte never had the privilege or the pleasure of a formal introduction, but she just couldn't believe he would be the one Margaret married.

A quick glance back at Margaret and Charlotte had her answer. The gleam in her friend's eyes and the broad smile on her face confirmed it.

"How did you ever manage that?" Charlotte stood in amazement. To think while she was occupied with running a bookstore, her friend had married into royalty. Well, almost. "You, of all people. Married to a baron from England." She shook her head. "This has to be the finest unveiling of the entire season."

"I am pleased to see you approve."

"How could I not?" As if she would ever begrudge anyone happiness, especially the kind that guaranteed her friend's future.

A momentary pang of melancholy crossed Margaret's face. "I have been the recipient of some rather malicious and vindictive remarks from a select few. But overall, the response and welcoming of my husband has been quite pleasant."

"As well it should be. Don't pay any attention to those who speak ill of you. They are merely jealous they weren't the ones to attract the attention of a baron." She reached out and clasped Margaret's hands. "You, my dear, are now a baroness, and you have earned every bit of the honor and grace the title bestows."

A shimmer of tears glistened in her friend's eyes. "Thank you. That truly means a lot to me," she said.

"You are quite welcome." Charlotte released Margaret's hands and turned back toward the double doors leading inside. She listened to the music floating on the air and tried to recall the order of the dances. "Now I believe I should make my way back to the ballroom so my next dance partner will be able to locate me."

"Very well." Margaret stepped forward and embraced Charlotte. "I do thank you for being supportive."

Charlotte returned the hug then stepped back. "My pleasure. Be sure and come find me before you depart so I might have a proper introduction to the baron." She winked. "And enjoy yourself this evening, Baroness," she added, stressing the final word.

"I shall."

How much fun it was to even say that word, let alone put it together with a young woman she'd known since the two of them were in pinafores and braids. She still couldn't believe it. A glance over her shoulder as she reached the double doors confirmed it wasn't a dream. As Charlotte watched, the baron joined Margaret on the terrace. If only she could be so fortunate.

Charlotte stepped into the ballroom and made her way around the perimeter. If she walked slowly, her next dance partner might have a better chance of locating her. She sidestepped one rather vigorous couple who danced in a wide arc from the rest; then she paused near one of the hallways leading into the rest of the manor. As she peered across the room, a low voice just beyond her right shoulder caught her ear.

"I cannot understand why Charlotte spends so much time attending these events and dressing in her finest." She'd recognize that voice anywhere. Amelia Devonshire. The mention of her name and the biting tone set Charlotte's senses on high alert. "It hasn't resulted in any success in previous seasons. Why would this year be any different?"

"It simply does not make sense," another female voice added, only this one didn't sound as petulant. "She is quite lovely, after all. I don't understand why most gentlemen barely give her a passing glance."

Charlotte wondered as well. It wasn't as if she made herself unappealing. And she'd heard from many others, including her mother, about her pleasing appearance. Some even went so far as to tell her she would be the belle of the ball. But so far, that had never proven true. What about her repelled eligible gentlemen?

"My dear, do you not know?" Amelia asked. "Charlotte owns a bookshop. That puts her in with the working class." Distaste dripped from her words. "We all know we are supposed to master the fine art of managing a household and learning our place in society. Working and owning a business does not fit with that plan."

Charlotte wanted to walk away, but morbid curiosity kept her feet planted where she stood. If nothing else, she wanted to determine the identity of the other two ladies keeping company with Amelia. Perhaps she'd discover something important if she allowed their conversation to play out.

"But I have known other young women who have married, and they also worked," a third voice said. "Why should Charlotte be any different?"

"Are you referring to Genevieve Chatterton or Margaret Howard?" A dismissing huff punctuated Amelia's words. "Or perhaps I should say Lady Margaret instead." Sarcasm laced every word.

"Yes," the second voice replied. "Margaret is a baroness now, and she spent a great deal of time working in her father's factory in Wilmington."

"Look at her tonight," the third lady added. "She appears every bit the refined lady, befitting her title."

"You can dress the part easily, but your garments cannot hide what lies underneath. And it's only a matter of time before Margaret's real identity shows itself."

Amelia should heed her own words. Charlotte didn't dare peer around the corner, but Amelia no doubt looked the part of the demure and charming lady. Yet hidden inside was a bitter soul. Charlotte might feel sorry for her if Amelia's biting remarks hadn't been directed at both Margaret and her. Perhaps Amelia was one of those people Margaret had mentioned moments ago. The ones who delivered malicious remarks.

"Still," the third voice continued, "I cannot see Charlotte being considered less than worthy in any way. She has always seemed generous, kind, and almost amiable to a fault."

"But she keeps her nose buried in her books and her bookshop," the second countered. "And that is no way to meet a potential suitor."

Charlotte almost smiled. If only they knew how much inaccuracy their estimations contained. Spending time in her bookshop had brought a very eligible bachelor into her life. Richard might not be an actual suitor, but he certainly possessed all the qualities of one.

"Lillian, I must disagree with you on that point. The bookshop is not deterring eligible gentlemen. Charlotte has a great deal to offer a potential beau. They merely have to spend a bit more time getting to know her first."

Charlotte gasped. Bethany! Why was she associating with ladies of that sort? Her own sister was standing there, allowing the other three ladies to discredit her name? And she waited until now to defend Charlotte's honor?

"You are only saying that because she is your sister," Amelia replied. "Mark my words. Charlotte Pringle will likely never marry. She will become a spinster, sequestered among the musty, lonely confines of her bookshop with nary a prospect for a secure future."

The room suddenly grew quite constricting. Charlotte had trouble catching her breath. Unbidden tears pooled in her eyes. She withdrew a handkerchief from her reticule and touched it to her nose. She had to get out of here. But the only exit necessitated walking directly past the hallway where those ladies stood. She could return to the veranda, but far too many people were already out there. She couldn't stay here or the tears would surely fall. Someone was bound to take notice.

Throwing caution to the wind, she kept the handkerchief in front of her face and faked a sneeze. Then she ducked her head and made a dash for the main door leading toward the front of the manor.

"Charlotte!"

Her sister's cry barely registered. She had to keep going, lest she lose her bravado and break down in front of an audience.

She rushed ahead, not taking time to look at the handful of people she passed on her way out.

"Charlotte, wait!"

Bethany's voice sounded stronger. She must be rather determined to chase after her in such a way. And Charlotte didn't want to think about the scene the two of them made.

Just as she made it to the front of the manor, a staff member opened the heavy oak door, allowing access over the final hurdle in her escape. She stepped onto the porch and inhaled a breath of fresh air. A moment later, a hand grabbed her arm and spun her around.

"Charlotte, I know you must have heard me," Bethany said. "Why did you not stop and wait for me?"

Charlotte looked through a blurry haze at her sister's concerned face. "Because I did not wish to make a scene in front of everyone in the ballroom."

Bethany gave a soft smile. "And you did not consider that running from the room with me attempting to catch you would cause a stir among our peers?"

Charlotte sniffed. "I didn't believe you'd come chasing after me."

Her sister took her hands and led her to a bench on the far

side of the porch. Once seated, she leveled a compassionate gaze at Charlotte. "I am truly sorry you had to overhear the cruel remarks Amelia made, and any bit of that conversation with Amelia, Clara, and Alice."

Charlotte dabbed at her eyes and sniffled. "I simply don't understand why they would say such things. What have I ever done to warrant their spite or bitterness?"

Her sister squeezed her hands. "Nothing. Nothing at all. Some ladies make it a practice to lash out at others to make themselves feel better. I don't believe I've ever heard Amelia speak kindly of anyone."

"And why were you there with them?" Her sister wasn't known for gossiping, and those young women weren't her friends.

"Believe me. It happened completely by accident." Bethany's eyes revealed nothing but sincerity. "I was speaking with Alice when Amelia and Clara approached. Since we stood at the end of the hallway, they had us pinned in the corner. . .literally." A faint smile appeared on her lips. "I was pleased to see you run away when you did, as it gave me a reason to escape, as well."

Charlotte should have known her sister wouldn't align herself with the likes of Amelia. "But the cruel things they said about Margaret and me. They have no reason to hurl such insults."

"No," Bethany said, sympathy in her voice. "But that does not mean they will change their ways."

Charlotte dabbed again at her eyes then blinked several times to clear her vision. "They accuse me of remaining sequestered in my bookshop. Why ever would I wish to leave the safety of those four walls when I end up encountering ladies like them?" Tucking her handkerchief back into her reticule, she called the faces of Richard and Grace to mind. "I'd much rather face unassuming individuals like Mr. Baxton and his niece Grace. They are so different from many who attend parties such as this one."

"And perhaps that is why you have your bookshop, sister dear." Bethany shifted on the bench and clasped Charlotte's hands tighter. "You do not belong within these social circles to find a beau."

A hollow laugh escaped from Charlotte. "Try persuading Mother of that."

Bethany nodded her understanding. "We shall have to address Mother some other time." A measured level of wisdom and concern filled Bethany's eyes. "For the time being, you need to remember God has a plan in all of this. Do not allow the words of those bitter women to upset you so. You have far more in your favor than they ever will. Focus on that, and the pain of their insults will fade into distant memory."

Wasn't she usually the one giving advice to Bethany and Anastasia? Yet here the two of them sat, the younger counseling the older. Charlotte pulled her hands free and embraced her sister. "Thank you."

Bethany returned the hug. "You are quite welcome." Leaning back, she again fixed an intent look upon her sister. "Now are we ready to return to the merriment? You cannot leave and allow those ladies to think they've achieved any measure of triumph at your expense."

A restorative laugh bubbled up from inside. "You are absolutely right."

Arm in arm, they went back inside and rejoined the revelry. But their conversation left Charlotte wondering one thing: Just when had her sister become so wise?

nine

Charlotte forgot Richard had offered to send one of his carriages, and she asked her own driver to prepare the horses then returned to the front hall to wait with her sister. A minute later, a knock came to the door, and when their butler opened it, there stood one of the Baxton carriages, ready and waiting to take her and Anastasia to Ashbourne Hills. How thoughtful of Richard to remember.

They rode together in silence with Anastasia staring out the window. That suited Charlotte just fine. She could center her thoughts on Richard. It hadn't been easy persuading Mother and Father to allow her to attend the party, but when she explained Anastasia was also invited, they had acquiesced. Perhaps they thought her sister would be more than willing to report back on all that transpired. Not that anything would. Far too many guests would be gathered for Charlotte to have any time alone with Richard. But she knew Mother and Father were just being concerned parents, looking out for her.

In no time, they'd traveled the almost nine miles to Richard's neighborhood and stopped in front of his home. Charlotte accepted the assistance of the footman as she descended onto the sidewalk. She approached the impressive home that had once belonged to Richard's brother. What had happened to the home Richard owned? Did he live there anymore, or did he sell it? She made a mental note to ask him another time.

Standing in front of the house for the first time, Charlotte studied the classic Colonial-style architecture with a hint of

Dutch influence. From Richard's clothing and the way he carried himself, she almost expected to see French accents as could be found in many of the major cities throughout America, or even the newer Renaissance revival style with a wide, covered front porch. But instead, this home remained true to some of the original settlers in the area. And it blended well with the other homes on the street.

"Impressive, isn't it?" The footman stood next to her and shared her view. When she looked his way, he took a step back and ducked his head.

"Yes, it is stunning," she said with a smile.

He seemed surprised she had replied, so he offered a smile in return. Another carriage approached. The footman glanced at it then extended his arm toward Charlotte while signaling another footman to escort Anastasia. But Charlotte remained on the front walk, transfixed by the beauty of the estate.

A handful of elm trees grew tall and protected the home set back about forty feet from the street. Two brick walks wound away from where she stood, one to the home and the other to the carriage house set farther back. It was near the end of June, and the wide variety of flowers planted out front blossomed in an array of colors, shapes, and sizes.

The footman cleared his throat, and Charlotte started.

"Oh! I am terribly sorry. You have other carriages that need your attention. Please forgive me for dawdling." She placed her hand in the crook of his arm and allowed him to escort her, with Anastasia and her footman close behind.

"It is quite all right, miss. Happens from time to time."

Many of the guests had likely already arrived, and she didn't wish to be tardy. They made their way down the brick path and ascended the five marble steps to the front porch where a butler swung wide the door.

"Miss Charlotte Pringle and Miss Anastasia Pringle," the

footman announced. The man bowed and took his leave.

A moment later, the butler ushered them inside. After taking their wraps, he directed Charlotte into the parlor to the right, but pointed Anastasia in another direction. Her sister disappeared with hardly a word, so Charlotte stepped into the other room. A maid wove her way through the other guests and held a tray of glasses filled with punch and various other beverages.

Charlotte took a glass of punch and sipped it as she blended in with the other guests and took time to observe the furnishings of the room. The faint sound of children laughing carried from one of the adjoining rooms. No doubt the pre-dinner fun and games for Grace's friends, Charlotte mused. That was likely where she'd find Anastasia, too. At least it seemed her sister would be having a great time. And Charlotte might too, once dinner was served. But this party wasn't for the adults. Most were likely there as chaperones or attending at Richard's request. So she again focused her attention on the décor.

The sofas and chairs were covered in crimson-and-black satin damask with their ends deeply tufted. The rosewood frames, delicately carved, had been polished until the wood gleamed. A grand piano sat in the corner where a young gentleman played soft strains of a pleasing melody. Even the satin drapes hanging from the doorway at the far end matched the crimson of the carpet under her feet. And the oval end tables were graced with sienna marble instead of the white slab her parents had.

The various decorative items placed here resembled their parlor, but the quality far outshone anything they had. Charlotte could only imagine the expense involved if the entire residence had been decorated in the same manner. The quality alone likely cost Richard's brother or father twice as much as what her parents had paid to decorate. The only aspects that seemed similar were the wallpaper patterns and the chandelier suspended from the ceiling in the center of the room.

She almost felt like an imposter. Her family had a great deal of wealth, but nothing compared to this. Yet for all the finery and obvious evidence of financial holdings, Richard and his niece remained genuine and approachable. They didn't allow their social status to affect how they treated others—one of many good points in their favor.

Still, it felt strange: recognizing that Richard's family must have spent a small fortune on these things, yet knowing he didn't have access to the money that would give his niece a much-needed operation. In many ways, it seemed unfair.

"It is sad, is it not," a woman standing next to Charlotte said, "to see such a finely decorated home and know of their struggle to settle the affairs following his brother's passing." She took a sip of her champagne and lowered her glass, the base clinking against the brooch pinned to her gown. With her left hand, she fingered the three rings on her right, each piece featuring a precious gemstone of a different color and cut. Even her finely coiffed hair was adorned with a delicate bejeweled tiara. "Why, it is almost as if they have nothing at all and are merely overseeing this home until the real owners return."

Charlotte wanted to ask why a woman like her didn't offer to donate something to Richard and his niece in order to help. But she didn't know the woman, and it would be rather impolite to pose such a question.

"Still," the woman continued. "I admire Mr. Baxton for seeing his niece receives the proper care and remains with family instead of one of those dreadful institutions in Wilmington or Philadelphia."

"Yes," Charlotte replied. "Not many would go to such great lengths. And little Grace is obviously benefiting from it."

The woman looked at Charlotte as if realizing for the first time she spoke with a stranger. "So, how did you come to meet Grace and her uncle?"

Charlotte hesitated before answering. How much should she tell to this woman? How well did *she* know the family? "I have had the good fortune of speaking with them on several occasions, but mostly Mr. Baxton. I have only spent a couple of hours with Grace."

"And what do you do, dear, that has led to your path crossing theirs?"

The woman seemed genuinely interested, and she hadn't yet given any indication that she might be less than trustworthy, so Charlotte decided to be completely honest.

"I own a bookshop in Brandywine, and Mr. Baxton has visited more than once to purchase books for Grace."

Recognition dawned in the woman's eyes. "Ah, so you're the bookshop owner I've heard so much about!" She set her near-empty glass on the tray as the maid walked by, then grabbed both of Charlotte's hands and gave them a squeeze. "I am very pleased to meet you, my dear. My name is Florence Lewis, but those who know me call me Flo." A twinkle entered her eyes as she released Charlotte's hands and leaned in close. "I used to be Richard and Elliott's nursemaid from the time they were in diapers to when they grew up on me and started their first jobs."

A woman who used to care for Richard and his brother as young lads certainly had to be honorable. "Charlotte Pringle, ma'am. I am pleased to meet you as well." But if she used to be a nursemaid, how was she now adorned with fine jewelry and able to afford an expensive gown?

"You are no doubt curious about my appearance," she said, laughing when Charlotte attempted to protest. "It is quite all right. I am often asked that very question. And the answer is that once the lads no longer needed me, I remarried and gained a rather substantial fortune." She waved her hand. "But enough about me. You say you own a bookshop in Brandywine?"

"Yes. Cobblestone Books. It is directly across from the east entrance to the park."

"I might just have to take a carriage ride out your way sometime." She gave Charlotte a conspiratorial wink. "See what all the fuss is about. Although after meeting you, I have a feeling it's about more than the books you sell."

Warmth stole into Charlotte's cheeks at the telling remark. Hearing this woman talk did make Charlotte wonder just what Richard—or possibly Grace—had said about her. She hadn't considered the possibility anyone would speak of her out here in Ashbourne Hills. Then again, why not? Any word spread would be good for business.

"Dinner is served, ladies and gentlemen," the butler announced. "Please make your way to the dining room."

Charlotte joined the flow of guests as they moved from the parlor and headed toward the dining room. If the first room had been impressive, this one was extraordinary. Several large mirrors with gilded frames flanked two of the walls. Large portraits of two rather distinguished gentlemen—who appeared to be Richard's father and grandfather—adorned the wall behind the head of the table, and three stately windows with brocade curtains were spaced a few feet apart on the fourth wall.

The polished mahogany table in the center of the room gleamed, and Charlotte could see the reflection of those already gathered around the table in its surface. More guests filtered in, but she held back. She seemed to be the only one unaccompanied.

"Miss Pringle!"

Grace's delighted voice rang out across the room, and all heads turned. Charlotte looked up to see the young girl wheeling herself in through a door opposite where she stood, her young friends trailing close behind. The adult guests followed the girl's line of focus and landed on her. Charlotte tried not to notice and kept her eyes on Grace.

"You came!" She maneuvered to the head of the table and pointed at two empty chairs to her left. "These seats are for you and Anastasia. I made a special request when I received your reply saying you would come tonight."

In the most unassuming manner she could manage, Charlotte made her way to the table and stood by her seat, making sure to put her sister directly to Grace's left. Grace beamed. Her reaction made the entire evening worthwhile. Yet she couldn't help but wonder about the other guests. How had she and Anastasia earned such a place of honor above everyone else? Surely someone like Flo or one of Grace's friends or even another family member should be sitting there. Then again, it seemed as if Grace's family occupied the seats on the other side of the table. A woman who had to be Grace's grandmother sat to Grace's right, putting Richard directly across from Charlotte. Flo was next in line. Not the order Charlotte would have expected, but who was she to be critical?

Her thoughts were once again interrupted by the arrival of their host, resplendent in dark trousers, a white ruffled shirt and black bow tie, and a dark coat with tails. Richard stood behind Grace and rested his hands on the back of her chair, then quickly scanned the faces of everyone seated at the table. When his gaze landed on Charlotte, he gave her a quick wink. She tried to keep the blush at bay, but she'd never seen him look so handsome.

"I'd like to thank everyone for coming this evening. You all know we are here to celebrate the joyous occasion of Grace's birthday." He moved his hands to his niece's shoulders. "All of you offered your support to us when we needed it most.

Thanks to that support, we are able to share together a special day for a very special girl." He looked down the table, his gaze resting on each guest on both sides of the table. "I couldn't think of a better way to thank you than to invite you and your families here to enjoy a delicious meal."

"Uncle Richard?" Grace twisted her neck and looked up at Richard. "Can I say a prayer before we begin?"

He squeezed her shoulders and smiled. "Of course. Would everyone please bow their heads?"

It was more a command than a request, but every guest complied. Charlotte added another quality to the growing list of desirable traits: Richard made no attempts to hide his faith from his guests, whether they believed or not.

"Dear Jesus, thank You for all these friends who came tonight to celebrate with me. Every one of them is special to me and to You. Thank You for putting them in my life and for their help after my accident. Please bless our dinner and this entire evening. In Your name, amen."

Murmurs of agreement and other rumblings sounded all the way down the table. Grace's words had clearly touched almost everyone there. Charlotte shifted her gaze to Richard. After pulling out his chair and taking a seat, he extended his arms toward his guests.

"Let's get this dinner under way."

Several footmen attended to the ladies present, reaching for the napkins on the table and fanning them out before placing them in the ladies' laps.

In a matter of moments, the soft din of voices rose from the table. Flo pressed against the table.

"My dear, I am quite pleased at the company in which I find myself. I cannot imagine a more enjoyable dinner companion." The woman shifted her attention to her left. "Richard, you have done a fine job in assigning the seats here at this end. I had the fortune of meeting Miss Pringle in the parlor just prior to being called to dine. And now I can not only discover more about her"—she cast a glance at Charlotte—"but I can also divulge some amusing stories about when this gentleman was a boy."

Richard raised one eyebrow in Flo's direction. "Now, now, Miss Flo." His amused tone belied the warning in his words. "Don't you go telling tales and destroying my carefully constructed respectable image. I shall never forgive you."

"Oh fiddlesticks." Flo waved off his protest. "You know very well I mean no harm. It shall all be in good fun."

"And I would love to hear stories again of Uncle Richard when he was my age," Grace chimed in.

Flo gave a single succinct nod, the mass of hair atop her head wobbling with the action. "And so you shall, sweet girl. So you shall."

Salads were placed in front of them, and they halted their conversation for a few moments. After waiting for everyone to be served, the guests looked to Grace to take her first bite. She did and Richard waved his fork in the air to encourage everyone else to do the same.

After eating her first forkful, Flo picked up where she left off. "Now, where shall I begin? Should it be with the time when your uncle and father painted one of the carriage horses a healthy shade of pink? Or perhaps the story of how they managed to escape their father at the shipyard in Wilmington and wound up dousing several torches along the main street."

Charlotte pressed her lips closed against the laughter. How embarrassing it would be if she spit out some of her food before she had a chance to swallow it.

Richard swallowed his recent bite and placed his right hand on his chest, fork held between his fingers. "In my defense, the painted horse was in honor of our mother who had read us a story about colorful animals. Elliott and I decided to give her a live one." He gave Flo a mock angry glare, but the twitching at the corner of his lips gave him away. "As for the torches, just be grateful the lamps still ran on fire or gas. By this time next year, we'll likely have electric street lamps in all the major cities and towns here in Delaware."

"Electric lights? Really?" a young lad spoke up from Charlotte's left. He must be a friend of Grace's, or at least a friend of the family to be sitting in such close proximity to Grace.

"Clarence! Mind your manners. You speak only when spoken to." The petite woman who must be Clarence's mother spoke in a firm hush then looked at Richard. "I am sorry, Mr. Baxton."

He dismissed her apology with a wave of his hand. "Think nothing of it, Mrs. Fillmore. Young Clarence here is merely excited. . .as we all are, no doubt. Electric lights will bring an air of distinction to our priLaura city and nearby towns." He glanced at Flo. "And mischievous boys won't be able to douse them out quite so easily."

Their salads were removed and replaced by steaming bowls of French onion soup. Charlotte eagerly sampled the delicious broth. Silence fell upon the table as many took their initial fill of the second course. A few minutes later, Flo resumed the conversation.

"Yes, but electric lights might present an entirely different level of temptation."

A man Charlotte assumed to be Mr. Fillmore made quick order of his soup and laid his spoon in the empty bowl, then rested his forearms on the edge of the table. "No more than the dynamite and nitroglycerin being manufactured by at least one of the Du Pont Company factories. If young lads succumb to the lure of mischief, they may be more fascinated by explosions than the buzz and hum of electric lamps."

"What do you think, Clarence?" Grace asked between sips of soup. "Would you prefer the electric lights or the dynamite?"

An impish grin played on his lips, matching perfectly with his unkempt and tousled hair. "I would definitely prefer the dynamite." He glanced across the table at his parents and composed himself like a dutiful son should. "But I would never play with something that dangerous. Besides," he said as he looked back at Grace, "there are more than enough ways to cause a little mischief right here in Ashbourne Hills."

Mr. and Mrs. Fillmore both shook their heads. Charlotte smiled down at Clarence and winked. He winked right back.

"You know," Richard spoke up. "Why don't we move Clarence here to the end of the table next to Grace." He looked at the two women who flanked his sides. "Mother? Would you ladies mind shifting down one seat to allow this young lad to be closer to the girls?"

"Not at all," Mrs. Baxton replied.

He smiled at his former nursemaid. "And Miss Flo? You could move to sit next to Charlotte."

"It would be my pleasure," Flo said with a mischievous grin as she, Clarence, Richard, and his mother played musical chairs.

"Clarence," Charlotte said once everyone was settled again, "you might consider reading *The Celebrated Jumping Frog of Calaveras County* by Mark Twain. I believe you will like it."

"Is that the same author who wrote about Tom Sawyer and Huckleberry Finn?"

"The very same." Charlotte finished her soup and patted her mouth with her napkin. "I have a copy in my bookshop in Brandywine, but you can likely find it right here in Ashbourne Hills at one of the shops in town."

Mrs. Fillmore nodded. "We shall look for it on our next shopping trip."

"And before long, even those trips will be more fun to make," Mr. Fillmore said.

"What do you mean?" Grace asked.

"Some of my colleagues serving on the state legislature have discussed bringing electric streetcars to Wilmington." He looked at his son. "With the city only two miles to the south, we should be able to ride in on them."

Grace straightened in her chair and grinned. "They sound like a lot of fun. Maybe even less bumpy than riding in a carriage."

"Just imagine," Anastasia added. "A carriage without horses. No more messy streets. And cars run by electricity. It's exciting!"

The girls' fascination with the modernized method of transportation was infectious. Charlotte had read stories and heard of reports from those who had ridden on the conveyances, but she had yet to experience it herself. Since the electric cars were rumored to replace the current horse-drawn ones, Charlotte had to admit a greater level of anticipation for what was to come.

The next part of their dinner was a refreshing serving of lime sorbet to cleanse their palates in preparation for the main course. Conversation stalled for just a moment as each of them took a small spoonful of the sweet treat.

From that point forward, talk continued to focus on the improvements being made in Wilmington and surrounding areas. Grace, Anastasia, and Clarence continued to focus on the streetcars, but the adults discussed efforts to become more like Philadelphia and everything that city had to offer. Conversation moved from the dinner table to the drawing room, where a substantial collection of wrapped gifts awaited Grace.

Charlotte was amazed at the warmth, love, and obvious support everyone showed toward Grace. It reminded her of her own family when her mother wasn't pushing her to fulfill social duties. And Grace's love of books was clearly not a secret. Nearly every gift she opened contained a book. What would that mean for visits by Richard to her shop? Would she see him less? Grace had enough books to keep her reading all summer and beyond.

"Don't worry, dear," Flo said from just behind Charlotte's shoulder. "Richard will find another excuse to travel to Brandywine."

How had Flo known the trail of her thoughts? Was Charlotte that transparent? As if he heard Flo's low-spoken words, Richard glanced up from his place next to Grace and looked directly at Charlotte. His eyes seemed to echo what Flo had just said, and again Charlotte questioned her own ability to keep her thoughts reined in.

Before she knew it, the evening had come to a close. Guests filtered out, each one extending their well wishes and congratulations to Grace on reaching the age of twelve. Charlotte could hardly believe Grace was only two years younger than Anastasia. Before long, the young girl would be looking to the social seasons and seeking a beau.

At that realization, Charlotte remembered Grace's circumstances and the chair where she sat. She had to do something to help. Perhaps an idea would come to her on the ride home. That thought made her realize it was time to depart. She and Anastasia had lingered long enough.

"Charlotte," Richard said just before she'd left the drawing room. He covered her right hand with both of his. "Thank you for coming tonight. You too, Anastasia. It meant the world to Grace."

Charlotte turned and looked up into eyes that showed his appreciation far more than his words. "It was our pleasure, Richard. We truly had a wonderful time. And I had the added bonus of meeting Flo." Charlotte grinned. "I'm happy we could be here for Grace."

"I'm happy you came as well." Sincerity and earnestness reflected in his gaze. "I look forward to seeing you again soon. And do not worry about the books Grace received tonight. I am certain she will take any opportunity to escape the confines of this house and go for a carriage ride. Perhaps next time we can take a walk by the creek."

"That sounds nice."

He raised her hand to his lips and placed a kiss on her knuckles. "Until next time." With a signal to the butler, he bowed and released her hand, never breaking his intent gaze. "I'll have my driver return you two safely home."

Charlotte could hardly breathe. Her hand tingled, and she longed for the warmth of his touch again. But that desire paled in comparison to the carefully controlled emotion she caught in his expression. A part of her wanted to remain and explore it further, but the wiser side recognized the prudence in leaving. She and her sister turned, only to almost stumble over Grace in her chair.

The girl watched Charlotte closely, a smile tugging at the corners of her mouth. "Miss Pringle, thank you again. You and Anastasia made tonight extra special." She extended her arms upward. "May I give you a hug?"

Oh, the preciousness of such a darling young lady. "Of course you may." Charlotte kneeled and embraced Grace as well, placing a kiss on her forehead as she drew away. "Have a good night, Grace." She tapped the girl's nose and smiled. "We shall see each other again soon. I promise."

Grace looked between Charlotte and her uncle, a smile almost appearing and a special light in her eyes. "Good night, Miss Pringle."

Anastasia led the way, but before Charlotte left the room, she turned again for one last glance at the two people who had become so special to her. Something about the way

Grace said good night and how Richard now watched her set her heart thumping. Just what had the girl seen? And what thoughts lay hidden in Richard's mind?

A few moments later, she rested her head against the back wall of the carriage and relaxed her hands in her lap. Anastasia launched into a nonstop recounting of the evening, and Charlotte let her talk. Her sister didn't need anyone to reply, anyway. And it gave her time to get lost in her own thoughts. How did she fit into this entire experience? She firmly believed everything happened for a reason. While she might not be able to figure out that reason, she had a duty to give back out of her own abundance or bless others in need when she had something to offer. Grace had a need, and Charlotte had the resources to help. An idea started taking shape in her mind. God's Word said if she served those she encountered, she served as if unto Him. And she would do just that. Meeting remarkable people like Richard and Grace was just a bonus.

ten

"Can you believe it?" Margaret stood behind Charlotte's booth, arranging books and setting out others for a more eye-capturing display. "This must be the most successful bazaar I have ever attended. The abundance of merchants and tradesmen is simply splendid!"

Charlotte panned the area from left to right. Nearly fifty booths sat scattered on both sides of the walking path in the park. "I cannot disagree. When I circulated word of wanting to arrange this event, I had six or seven merchants respond almost immediately. They told other merchants, who told several businessmen, who also included tradesmen as well, and"—she twisted her hands around like a magician after performing a trick—"we have our bazaar in the park."

"It bears the markings of being both a rewarding and productive event." Margaret bent to retrieve a book that had fallen to the ground. She dusted it off and placed it on the table. "I should not be surprised if you achieve your goal of the full amount for Grace's surgery from this one day alone."

"Perhaps." Charlotte prayed it would happen, but she wouldn't know until the day ended. "But even if I fall short of my goal, I am both pleased and amazed at the diversity and array of options available to all passersby."

"And participating vendors as well," Margaret pointed out. "Although I would have to say the most comical booth is the one featuring the two costumed thespians acting out scenes from their latest play."

"That was one booth I eagerly welcomed when they approached me last week. I felt it an ingenious way of

114

advertising the theatre company in Wilmington."

"It certainly brings a sense of merriment to an otherwise merchant-focused affair."

"Consider me a soft heart. The owner told me they are attempting to raise enough money to invest in a building they can own instead of being forced to make use of whatever unused stage they are able to find. Wilmington will benefit greatly from an actual playhouse where everyone can go to see the many plays being performed. How could I deny him that opportunity?"

"You can't." Margaret touched Charlotte's shoulder and smiled. "And I applaud you for allowing them to participate. An excellent decision."

Charlotte looked down at the table and picked up her ledger recording the day's sales. She knit her brows. "Forgive me for changing the subject so abruptly, but did we sell the copy of *Gulliver's Travels*? I do not see it here, and I know it is not marked in my ledger." She glanced at Margaret. "Do you recall if you sold it earlier today?"

Margaret bit her lower lip. "Yes, I did. And I forgot to write it down. Three other customers stood ready to make purchases, and I am afraid it slipped my mind."

"It's all right. As long as between the two of us we remember." Charlotte grinned. "But if it happens again, I shall subtract some of your wages."

Her friend raised one eyebrow. "A difficult feat to accomplish considering you are not compensating me." Margaret came ready to work in a simple walking dress, but even the quality of the cotton material gave evidence to her fairly recent rise in station. "However, I am going to make it a point to pay a visit to several booths should you permit me a period of rest from my work."

Charlotte sniggered but attempted to compose herself. She leveled her best reprimanding glance. "And what, pray tell, makes you believe you have earned a rest?" She made a sweeping gesture with her right arm. "We have only reached the halfway point of this event. And I might be called upon to see to other details. That would leave my booth unattended. We cannot have that happen, now can we?"

Margaret picked up on her jesting. "Oh, of course not. But should you be called away, I cannot promise that I will not find a random passerby to oversee the booth in my absence."

"So long as there is someone here at all times." Charlotte shrugged. "Who am I to be particular about the identity of that person?" She smiled and moved to straighten a stack of books. "Besides, far be it from me to tell a baroness she is not permitted to have a well-deserved rest. I wouldn't wish to risk the wrath of Baron Edward James Heddington of Sutherland. He might have me tarred and feathered."

With surprising speed, Margaret whipped out her fan and smacked Charlotte on the upper arm. "You are positively irredeemable. To think, my husband ever ordering such barbaric punishment." She tapped her fan to her chin. "Although I cannot guarantee the whipping post or pillory would be out of the question."

The two women dissolved into a fit of laughter at the absurdity of their conversation. At least the day would pass by more quickly than if Charlotte had been working the table by herself.

A lady with two well-dressed children approached their booth, so Charlotte quickly composed herself. "Good afternoon, ma'am. How may we help you?"

The lady nodded and her daughter curtsied while her son bowed. Children with impeccable manners! Charlotte didn't often see that in the park.

"Good afternoon," the lady replied. She glanced at Charlotte, then at Margaret, and jerked her head back to look again. "Oh! Good afternoon, Baroness. I had no idea you would be in attendance today."

Margaret regarded the lady and pursed her lips. "Do forgive me, but are we acquainted from another event, or might we have been introduced elsewhere? If so, I cannot seem to recall your name."

Charlotte raised her eyebrows at her friend, who didn't seem to notice. Where had the jovial woman who had only moments before been making light of whipping post punishments gone? In her place was a dignified, proper lady with a rather refined manner of speech. Charlotte was amazed at the quick transformation.

The lady waved her hand in dismissal. "No apology is necessary, Baroness. In fact, I would be quite surprised if you recalled me at all." Margaret remained confused, so the lady rushed ahead. "My name is Elizabeth Frederick, and I was in attendance at your wedding to the Baron a few months past. You see, my cousin is the nephew of your husband's uncle."

Understanding dawned on Margaret's face. Charlotte, on the other hand, tried to make the connection. So, this lady's cousin was also a cousin of Margaret's husband.

The lady continued. "We are here from Philadelphia visiting my sister, and she mentioned this bazaar." She placed one hand on each of her children's shoulders in loving affection as she glanced down at them. "I told William and Louise here we would take some time to come. They were quite impressed with the theater pair. But I saw this booth with books and felt compelled to stop." She smiled at Margaret. "Now, I am rather delighted I did."

Margaret smiled in return. "I shall be certain to tell the baron of our meeting here today. He will no doubt be pleased to hear of it." She switched personas and became a saleswoman. "Now, is there something in particular you are seeking, or would you like me to make a suggestion?"

Charlotte chose that opportunity to leave and start her

rounds. Her booth was in capable hands, and she'd likely have a sizable sale upon her return. Time to check the rest of the vendors and how their sales had gone so far.

A little over an hour later, Charlotte finished with the final vendor and tallied the results. A broad smile formed on her lips. Praise the Lord! Her goal had been reached. And the day hadn't yet concluded. Who knew how much there'd be by day's end. So many generous merchants and craftsmen. Without prodding, each one of them had agreed to donate half of their proceeds to Grace's need. They had simply heard of her plan and volunteered to be involved. A successful bazaar indeed. Just as Margaret predicted. Now Grace could have her operation.

Charlotte could hardly wait to tell Richard and Grace.

❧

"Uncle Richard, look!" Grace pointed across the creek to a red-crowned crane wading about thirty feet away. "A crane. I cannot believe I saw a crane."

"Excellent observation, Grace." Richard walked behind her, pushing the wheeled chair over the dirt path along the creek's edge.

They had met Charlotte at her bookshop about twenty minutes ago and made their way down through the tulip poplars, giving them a great deal of shade on this sunny afternoon. From the moment he saw Charlotte, he'd noticed a certain light in her eyes and extra bounce to her step. What had happened since Grace's birthday party to make her so cheerful? She must have received good news of some kind. Perhaps another rare book she treasured. Or maybe higher sales than expected at her bookshop. He hoped she'd tell them today.

"You should have your notepad and pencil with you, Grace, so you can write down the different species you see today. Then you could write a special report to include with your daily studies. Your tutor would be quite impressed."

"I don't need paper." Grace tapped her head near her right temple. "I remember it all up here."

Richard glanced at Charlotte as she walked next to them. "Says the girl who had difficulty recalling the name of the substantial land purchase President Jefferson made earlier in the century. Right about the time the du Pont family emigrated here and had heavy influence with Jefferson and France." Grace usually demonstrated a rather keen intelligence when it came to history. Something else must be on her mind. Much like Charlotte. He still wanted to know when she'd say something.

"Do you mean the Louisiana Purchase?" Charlotte asked.

Obviously not now. And he wasn't about to initiate the discussion. He'd leave it up to her.

"One and the same." Richard patted Grace's head. "This one thought it was the Lewis and Clark Territory."

"Well, they *were* the ones to explore the land and report back with their maps, notes, and charts. It could easily be an honest mistake."

Grace turned and gave a broad smile, showing her appreciation for Charlotte defending her. She then stuck her chin in the air and harrumphed. The corners of Charlotte's lips turned down as she attempted to hide her grin. Somehow, Richard felt like the odd man out in this trio. For the moment, Charlotte was the champion and he the accuser.

"All right," he continued, forcing a teasing tone into his voice. "What about the name of the man who was responsible for claiming Delaware for the British?"

Grace folded her arms and looked straight ahead. He could imagine the frown on her face, or even the pout. With a quick bend at the waist, he leaned forward and peered over her shoulder. Sure enough, the frown and pout were both there.

"Grace," Charlotte chided, "you couldn't recall William Penn?"

"I only remembered him for founding Pennsylvania." She twisted in her chair as best she could and wrinkled her nose up at Richard. "At least I remembered Lord de la Warr."

Richard took a step closer to Charlotte and lowered his voice. "She isn't very good at accepting constructive criticism or correction when she makes mistakes."

Charlotte pressed her lips together, showing one dimple where the corner of her mouth crooked, and raised her eyebrows as if shrugging. "Do you know anyone who is?"

He made a quick jab, mimicking a parry with a sword. "Touché."

She grinned. "I believe Grace is perfectly justified in her indignation when someone chides her about those mistakes. Just remember all the facts she gets right and allow her a slip or two now and then."

"All right. I see your point." He probably shouldn't have teased his niece in front of Charlotte. But it wasn't easy remembering her young and impressionable age all the time. She seemed so much older in most instances and conversed with him, often better than many adults he knew. Again, he lowered his voice, placing one of his hands over his chest. "I promise I shall endeavor to be more lenient to my niece when the situation warrants it."

His antics caused Charlotte to laugh as she shook her head. "And I thought Grace was the impish one among us."

He shrugged. "Let us just say she comes by it honestly."

Charlotte took a deep breath then opened her mouth to say something, but Grace spoke first.

"Miss Pringle, what is on the other side of the creek?"

Yet another missed opportunity. Richard sighed. How long would they have to wait? At least Charlotte's eyes hadn't lost their excitement. But now he was getting anxious.

Charlotte turned her head in the direction Grace pointed. Several identical barns sat side by side not too far from the main house. "Oh, that's a dairy farm owned by the du Pont family. They only recently built these stone walls you see wending their way across the rolling hills."

"There are more cows than I can count. I guess that means they get a lot of milk every day."

Now it was Richard's turn to laugh, and Charlotte looked over at him with an amused expression. "She *is* quite astute, as you pointed out a few moments ago."

"Yes," Richard replied. "She is that. I am not certain how I will ever keep up with her if she continues to excel at this rate."

"Well, keeping up with her might be more of a challenge than you imagine."

"Pardon me?"

Charlotte looked out across the creek, silent for several moments. When would she share her news with them? A few more moments passed, but she didn't say anything.

"Charlotte?"

She shook her head as if to clear it. "Why don't we rest for a bit and sit on the bench over there?"

"That sounds like an excellent idea." Richard tried not to sound too enthusiastic, but it seemed whatever Charlotte was about to tell them was quite important. And he wanted to know right now.

Once seated, she turned to face him and Grace, who sat between them in front of the bench. His niece's face also showed a keen interest in the conversation.

"I wanted to tell you both as soon as you arrived at the shop. But it didn't seem like the right time. I've been plagued by your predicament for quite some time."

Charlotte fidgeted with her hands, her eyes going from Richard to Grace to her lap and back again. Her eyes lacked the light they'd had for most of their walk. Instead, he saw only uncertainty and hesitation in them.

"I suppose there is only way to tell you, and that's straight out."

She reached into a hidden pocket of her skirts and withdrew a long envelope. Richard glanced down to see his name and Grace's on the front. He looked up at Charlotte and knit his brows. Predicament? Did she mean Grace's operation? Surely this wasn't a loan. If it was, he would refuse.

She held up the envelope, just out of his reach. "Now before you say anything, this isn't a loan. It is a collection of sorts."

"A collection?"

Once again, her face brightened, and the spark of excitement returned. "Yes. After Grace's birthday party, an idea came to me on the carriage ride home. I set to work right away, and before I knew it, I had managed to coordinate one of the largest bazaar's this area of town has ever seen."

"What's a bazaar?" Grace asked.

Charlotte smiled. "It is a gathering of local merchants, tradesmen, and other professionals who set up booths and sell or showcase something related to their line of work."

Richard pointed at the envelope. "And this bazaar is how you managed to take up the collection?"

"Well, partially." She covered the envelope with her other hand. "Only half the proceeds from the vendors is in this envelope. The rest they retained for their time and their trade." A substantial look of satisfaction reflected in her eyes as she handed the envelope to Richard. "And I want you and Grace to have it. There is more than enough money inside to cover the surgery and any additional expenses incurred as a result."

Grace watched the exchange and looked back and forth between her uncle and Charlotte. "Miss Pringle, why are you giving us money?"

Richard remained silent, overwhelmed. He could only stare at the envelope. Tucked inside was the answer to weeks and months of prayer. How in the world could he ever thank her?

Charlotte leaned forward and took Grace's hands in hers. "Because, sweetheart, I want you to be able to have that operation."

"Really? Do you truly mean it? The money is for me?"

Charlotte laughed. "Yes, dear one. Now nothing stands in your way."

Richard looked at his niece. Tears of joy pooled in her eyes and fell to her cheeks. She leaned forward and pulled Charlotte into an emotional embrace.

"Thank you! Thank you, thank you, thank you. This is the best surprise you could ever give us."

"Yes," Richard croaked. Just great. Where had his voice gone? Emotion tightened the muscles in his neck. He coughed and cleared his throat several times before continuing. "Grace is correct. This gift is quite amazing."

Charlotte leaned back from Grace and met his gaze. As he stared at her, he couldn't think of anything else to say. Words hardly seemed enough in a situation like this. What he wanted to do, he couldn't. Not only was Grace present, but he hadn't made his intentions known to Charlotte, and he wasn't about to overstep the bounds of propriety. Waiting until after something was official would be too late. He had to do something now.

Throwing caution to the wind, he reached for Charlotte's hands and placed a single kiss on the knuckles of each. Then, with a slight tug, he pulled her toward him and kissed her smooth cheek. When he leaned back and gauged her reaction, all he wanted to do was draw her into his arms. From the look in her eyes, her thoughts were close to his. But they had a rather impressionable audience. Grace was already too keen for her own good, and who knew what she'd make of this little exchange? At his first opportunity, he was going to arrange to speak to Charlotte's father.

Charlotte reached up and touched her cheek where he'd kissed it. She smiled at him.

He grinned. "I suppose saying thank you now is a rather moot point."

"Yes, but this other method is equally effective." Her sense of humor had returned.

"It appears Grace and I have some plans to make." He stood and pivoted Grace in her chair. Charlotte stood beside them. They started off in silence and walked several hundred feet. It was all so overwhelming. What could he say or do to get the conversation going again? Ah yes. Richard thought of something.

"All right, Grace. What do you remember so far from what you saw along the path and even in or near the creek?"

"Hmm. I remember the crane and the white-tailed deer." She tilted her head and looked up to the right. "Oh, and then there was the snapping turtle, the dragonflies, and the beautiful red-tailed hawk. I look forward to drawing him."

"Excellent." Richard squeezed both of her shoulders. "You should be aptly prepared to impress your tutor in grand fashion."

Grace chattered on about the wildlife as Richard pushed her chair along. Charlotte remained silent. He wished he could reach out and take her hand, but he needed both of his to steer and push Grace. So, he did the next best thing. . .put her hand on one of the handles and placed his hand on top.

She startled and looked up at him, but she didn't resist. Instead, she smiled, never breaking her stride. As they reached the cobblestone street in front of the bookshop, Grace stopped the wheels and brought the three of them to a halt.

"Miss Pringle, you will be there, won't you? At the hospital when I have my operation?"

"Of course I will. I would not want to miss that day for anything in the world."

Grace gave a succinct nod. "Good."

Richard continued to lead them to the bookshop. This day had turned out far better than he ever could have imagined. Charlotte hadn't backed away from his affectionate overtures. He and Grace had immediate access to the funds they needed for her operation. Grace just might walk again. And he would be speaking with Charlotte's father within the fortnight. How could things be any better?

eleven

Charlotte sat on the same bench in the park where she had sat with Richard not so long ago. A colorful array of wildflowers grew all around, providing a rainbow's splash to the otherwise green landscape. She glanced down at the letter in her hand for at least the tenth or eleventh time. Life for Richard and Grace had been extremely hectic since their walk by the creek.

Three weeks had passed, and she had three letters from them updating her on the countdown to the day of the operation. This latest one, though, was her favorite.

It began in the obvious hand of Richard, although she could see Grace's influence as well:

Dearest Charlotte,

We are only one week away from the scheduled surgery. And we would not have been able to get this far were it not for you. I realize we have expressed our gratitude many times over, but our hearts remain forever thankful for the time and effort you invested in order for us to receive the bountiful blessing God provided through your service.

Your treasured gift was a distinct answer to prayer, and it helped us remember that God has not forgotten about us. I confess our faith had wavered several times following the accident. Now, however, we are relying on our Lord's strength, and with dear friends such as yourself, we have everything we need.

Then the writing changed to Grace's:

I am a little frightened about the operation, but Uncle Richard has said he will be there the entire time. You will too, I hope. It will help if I can hold your hand and see your face, even though you cannot be in the room with me until the doctor is all done. This is going to be one of the best days of my life, and I want to share it with both you and Uncle Richard. Only one week until I see you again. I hope the days pass quickly.

The letter concluded with Richard's parting words.

This week may very well be difficult, but thinking of you will aid in its quick passing. Before we know it, we shall be awaiting the outcome from the doctor, and I am confident we shall rejoice with a successful operation. Please continue your prayers for us and for the doctor, as well as the attending nurses. Come Thursday, my carriage will be waiting to bring you to us. Until then, we remain your friends.

Sincerely,
Richard & Grace

Only one more week. As promised, she would continue to pray for all involved. Beyond that, however, Charlotte prayed she could be what they both needed on what was sure to be a difficult day. For Grace to want her by her side meant more than words could say.

A warm breeze rustled through the tulip poplars towering above the path. It whispered through the waist-high rushes along the creek banks. Charlotte closed her eyes and soaked in the sounds of nature. From the trills of the various songbirds to the splash of the trout and bluegill, to the crickets hiding in the grass and the occasional high-pitched cry of the red-tailed hawk, the musical symphony bore clear evidence of God's handiwork. It again reminded Charlotte the Lord was with her, and He'd be with Grace throughout her procedure.

❧

The soft murmur of voices traveled into the front hallway as Charlotte made her way toward the sitting room. Father had left word with their butler, asking to speak with her. From the sounds coming out of the room, Mother was present as well. It must be something significant for her to be summoned immediately upon arriving home. Whatever they had to say, she prayed it wouldn't be something she didn't want to hear. Before she stepped into view, she took a deep breath and willed her heart to settle down to a more even pace.

"Ah good," Mother announced as soon as Charlotte walked into the room. "Please, dear, come take a seat and join us."

Charlotte's feet sank into the woven carpet as she headed straight for her favorite settee. Her parents waited in the wingback chairs opposite her and presented the image of relaxation. Father leaned back in his chair and rested his hands on the arms. Mother tucked her legs underneath her, with her hands folded in her lap. When neither of them said anything, Charlotte swallowed and wet her lips.

Finally, Father spoke. "Before we get to the priLaura reason for asking to speak with you, your mother and I want to say how proud we are of the success you've had with your bookshop."

"Yes," Mother added, though Charlotte could tell her agreement came with resignation. "We have heard glowing reports from many of our friends, saying how much they love to visit your shop."

Charlotte didn't know how to respond. Complimenting her obviously wasn't the purpose of this conversation. She appreciated them making a point to begin with that though. Still, anticipating what might come next made her heart race.

Father again resumed control. "Now, for the matter at hand."

There was a matter? Charlotte crossed her right ankle over her left. She slowly smoothed her hands on the folds of her skirt. It helped absorb the dampness of her palms as she awaited Father's next words.

"Charlotte, you know your mother and I only want the best for you. But before we present a possible opportunity to you, there is something we must know."

Father leaned forward and clasped his hands together, resting his forearms on his knees. "We know you have been spending additional leisure time with a certain gentleman who has been frequenting your bookshop. And you have already told us of the forthcoming operation for the gentleman's niece." He met her gaze, but she couldn't read his expression. "Mr. Baxton has paid me a visit recently, and we had an enlightening chat."

Richard had been here? And he hadn't told her? This must have happened last week when she was attending the Ridenour Cotillion. Charlotte was surprised he'd accepted her mother's invitation to dinner without her knowing. She wished her parents had said something earlier.

"With that in mind," Father continued, "we'd appreciate your honest answer to the following question."

She knew what was coming. Even so, she didn't think she could provide an answer that would satisfy her parents. At least not with certainty.

Her father pinned her with an unwavering stare. "What are your feelings regarding Mr. Baxton?"

There it was. The question she knew they would ask. Charlotte opened her mouth to speak, but no words came out. She swallowed twice and tried to gather her thoughts. Considering Richard more than a friend had only recently occupied her thoughts. Now her parents expected her to make sense of her feelings and put them into words?

"Charlotte, dear," Mother interjected, breaking the silence. She peered into her daughter's face. "Do you simply not know how you feel?"

Clearing her throat, Charlotte tried again. "Father, Mother, I must confess. Up until a couple of weeks ago, Mr. Baxton and I were nothing more than friends. Other than attending the birthday party for his niece and our recent walk by the creek, nearly every one of our conversations has centered on Grace, his niece."

"And now?" Father pressed.

"Now?" She wet her lips again. "Now I don't know. I admit he has several appealing qualities about him, and I *am* attracted. Any more than that, I don't believe I can say for certain."

There. She might not have given them the response they sought, but she had been honest.

Father angled his body toward Mother and raised his eyebrows. Mother nodded in response. Charlotte sat in silence, awaiting what felt like a sentencing, even if that was a rather substantial exaggeration.

Finally, Father returned to his original position. "We appreciate your honesty, especially when you could have misled us or given us an answer merely to pacify us." His expression brightened, and he again sat back in his seat. "With that matter settled, we're faced with the issue of the time you spend with eligible men."

Did that mean they didn't consider Richard eligible because of his current state of affairs? Her heart fell, and her shoulders dropped. Were the social engagements not enough? She couldn't be faulted for the men not taking an interest in her. On the heels of asking her about Richard, though, it was clear where her parents stood.

Mother sat up straighter, eagerness replacing the previous concern. "We have been speaking with several of our friends and believe we've found one gentleman we'd like you to meet. He is poised to assume solid positions both in his father's footsteps and in a venture he's begun on his own."

So they *did* consider this gentleman more eligible than Richard. She wished she could muster up a bit more excitement in response to this announcement. Although she couldn't say for certain where she and Richard stood, she wasn't eager to pursue a possible romantic entanglement with someone else. Nevertheless, her parents had gone to some trouble on her behalf, and as their daughter, she owed them her respect and cooperation.

Father tilted his head in her direction. "Is there anything you'd like to say?"

Charlotte took a deep breath. "I must confess this comes as a surprise. I am sure you have my best interests at heart," she added with a soft smile. Best to do what she could to set them at ease. "I'm well aware my friends are all married or engaged. And I'm grateful you have been more patient regarding my arrangements."

"We're well aware of what can come of wanting to force certain outcomes," Mother replied. "Our family has a history of somewhat meddlesome parents. Even though the pairings worked out for the best, we agreed we didn't want to do the same to you."

"I appreciate that, Mother. But I suppose it *is* time for me to take the matter of my future more seriously." She looked at them before continuing. "You've both given me so much. How could I not honor your wishes?" Maybe with this shift in her priorities, she could continue to explore the possibilities with Richard, as well.

"Where Mr. Baxton is concerned," Father said, "we must caution you. He comes from a well-established family with a solid and successful business. But at present, there is no guarantee his situation will work out to his benefit. And we do not wish to see you hurt."

What? Just when she thought her parents were providing the perfect opportunity for her to discover the answers to all her questions about Richard, Father warned her against him?

"But, Father, it isn't like that at all." She unclasped her hands and extended them in a placating gesture. "I already said he is only a friend." At the moment, that much was true in reality. "Are you saying I can no longer spend any time with him or his niece?"

Father pressed his lips into a thin line. "What I am saying is prolonged interactions with him on a social level might prevent you from seeing possibilities with the other gentlemen you meet."

He hadn't set Richard apart from the class of a gentleman. That had to be something. Perhaps she could discover more about why he was facing such difficulty with his business and if he knew when it would all be resolved.

Mother nodded and pursed her lips. "I do not see any cause to end your associations with Mr. Baxton, Charlotte, dear. But I agree with your father. There are more than enough young men right here in the Brandywine area who I'm sure will provide a suitable distraction."

Mother didn't come right out and say it, but Charlotte could read between the lines. It wasn't that Richard might distract her from the other men. It was where he lived and his unknown financial status. Well, at least they hadn't forbiddin any association with him. They were only expressing their desire for her to be careful. That she could do.

"Thank you, Mother. Father." She regarded them each in turn and dipped her head in acknowledgment, maintaining a polite exterior. "I promise as soon as Grace's operation is over next week, I will devote appropriate attention to the potential suitor you have mentioned. We can discuss this further then, and you can arrange an introduction."

Her parents both stood, seeming pleased with Charlotte's promise.

"That is all we ask, dear," Mother said.

"Now let's adjourn to the dining room where I'm sure Laura has an appetizing meal ready."

Charlotte allowed her parents to precede her from the sitting room. That conversation hadn't gone as she preferred. It could have been much worse though. At least she was still permitted to spend time with Richard. But she only had a little more than a week. If anything more was to happen with Richard, God would have to work a miracle. She had to trust Him and leave it at that.

❧

"Charlotte!" Richard's anxious voice greeted her as soon as she stepped through the swinging double doors. "I'm glad you are here." He took a firm hold of her arm and started to pull her in the opposite direction.

She resisted, and he paused. "Wait a moment. Why is there such a sense of urgency?" Her right hand went to her chest. "Has something happened to Grace? Is she all right?"

"Grace is fine. But the surgeon arrived early this morning, and he wants to begin right now. I told him he couldn't until you arrived. Grace wants to see you before they wheel her into the other room." Richard resumed his tug on her arm. "Now, come with me."

They entered a stark white room almost identical to the rest of the hospital, except this room was furnished with two rose-hued chairs and a colorful patchwork quilt on the bed. Someone had thought ahead. A splash of color always brightened the spirit.

"Miss Pringle, you're here!" Grace's smile lit up the room. She tried to sit up, but the exertion took too much effort.

Charlotte rushed forward. "No, no. Please, Grace. Rest."

A nurse in starched uniform stood on the other side of the

bed. "We have only just sedated her with chloroform, but it should be taking effect any minute. If you have something you wish to say to her, you should do it quickly. Otherwise, she will not be able to respond."

Grace extended a hand toward Charlotte. "Miss Pringle, will you pray with me?"

Tears welled in Charlotte's eyes. "Of course I will, dear." She looked over her shoulder at Richard, and he nodded, stepping with her to Grace's bedside.

The young girl reached first for her uncle's hand and then for Charlotte's. She waited and looked back and forth between them both. Before Charlotte could figure out why Grace hesitated, Richard's fingers brushed hers in a silent request to take her hand. Ah, so that was it. Grace wanted their prayer circle to be complete. How could she deny the precious girl such an honest request?

As soon as Charlotte moved her fingers, Richard's hand enveloped hers, the warmth of his grasp traveling up her arm and straight to her heart. They all bowed their heads.

"Dear Jesus, thank You for bringing Miss Pringle here today, and thank You for the doctor who will be working to help me walk again. Thank You for the nurse to help the doctor and for Your blessing on us. Be with all of us, Lord, through everything that will happen today, and keep us safe. No matter what happens, we love You, and we know You love us. Amen."

Grace's words softened as her prayer drew to a close, and her grip loosened. She managed to open her eyes, though, and look right at Charlotte.

"I am happy you came," she said, sounding sluggish.

The nurse stepped forward as another attendant entered the room. "We need to take her now."

As the bed on wheels passed by Charlotte, Grace reached out again and touched her hand.

"I love you," she murmured.

Charlotte's eyes widened. Had she heard correctly? She looked at Grace, at the soft smile on the girl's lips. Yes, she must have. A warm hand touched her right shoulder, and Charlotte turned to see Richard with affection reflecting in his gaze. Quick. She had to do or say something in response to Grace. She touched two fingers to her lips and touched them to Grace's forehead.

"I love you, too, Grace."

The girl didn't respond, but her smile remained. At least Charlotte could send Grace into surgery knowing her love was returned. Now they just had to wait.

❧

Charlotte stood to stretch. Four hours. And in all that time, they had spoken only twice—when a nurse came to provide updates on the procedure. Other than that, they had been left alone in an alcove outfitted with two sets of benches opposite each other. There had been plenty of time for Charlotte to tell Richard about her recent conversation with her parents. She wanted him to know she knew about his visit to her father as well. But the moment wasn't right. Several times she started to open her mouth only to close it and remain silent.

Richard paced from one end of the benches to the other. In between paces, he cast a worried glance down the hall toward the operating room.

"Richard," Charlotte said, keeping her voice soft and free of chastisement. "The nurse was here only twenty minutes ago, and she reported everything being good. I know this isn't easy, but we have to have faith and trust God to be with Grace and the doctor now."

He halted his pacing and stared at her. Then his eyes closed, and a deep sigh escaped his lips. "You are right. My walking back and forth or looking down the hall isn't going to make the doctor finish any faster." He sat on the bench again, and

Charlotte joined him. Running his fingers through his hair, he slumped and rested his forearms on his thighs. "I just feel so incredibly helpless. I wish I could do something."

Compassion filled Charlotte. She started to reach out and touch his hand but retracted. What would he think of her? Would he consider her too forward? He had always initiated the gestures of physical touch. But he was in no frame of mind right now to do so. Charlotte swallowed and tried to calm her rapidly beating heart. What could it hurt?

Slowly, she shifted the few inches to her right to close the distance between them. Then she eased her hand toward him and covered his folded hands hanging at his knees. He didn't react.

"There is something we can do," she said. "We can continue to pray. That is the best help we can give to the doctor, to ourselves, and to Grace."

Richard looked up, his face bearing evidence of the strain. But as he gazed into her eyes, his expression changed. His mouth relaxed, his eyebrows smoothed, and a light entered his eyes. He withdrew one of his hands and clasped hers between his.

"You are absolutely right. Thank you. I could use the reminder."

"Sometimes we all can."

Together, they bowed their heads and prayed silently. Charlotte had no idea how long they remained that way, but she didn't care. She was there for Richard when he needed her most.

"Ahem."

Charlotte and Richard both looked up at the sound of a man clearing his throat. The doctor! Could that mean. . . ? Richard squeezed her hands.

"Mr. Baxton, I have finished with your niece's procedure. I believe the operation was a success." He held up his hands as if to stop someone from rushing forward. "Now obviously we won't know for certain until she wakes, and there will be a substantial amount of time for recovery. She has been without the use of her legs for several months. Her muscles are going to need to be strengthened, and she is going to have to learn how to use them all over again. It is going to be a difficult road for her. . .and you. And there remains a possibility the operation won't create a permanent cure. But we will be certain Grace receives the highest level of care for the duration of time she is with us."

Charlotte appreciated the doctor speaking to them in terms they could understand. At least she could follow this report.

Richard stood and extended a hand to the doctor. "Thank you, Doctor," Richard said. "We owe you a lot, regardless of the results."

The doctor shook his hand and offered a weary smile. "It was my pleasure. If I can help young Grace recover even part of the sensation in her limbs, I will consider this operation a success. But we are hoping for much more." The man looked back down the hall. "Now, if you will excuse me, I need to return to the operating room and tidy up a few things. We will speak with you soon about the next steps."

As soon as the doctor departed, Richard turned to face Charlotte, excitement spread across his entire face. Charlotte shared his enthusiasm. She wanted to shout out and rejoice. But Richard beat her to it.

He smiled and spread his arms wide. "He did it!"

"Yes. The operation was a success!" Without thinking, Charlotte threw her arms around Richard's neck. He wrapped his arms around her back and swung her in a circle then set her down. Almost immediately, Charlotte realized what they had done. Heat warmed her face, and she attempted to step away. But Richard held fast. She looked up at him, and his eyes darkened with an emotion that both compelled her and frightened her. He wanted to kiss her. And she wanted him to do it.

His hands tightened around her waist, and he lowered his head. Charlotte held her breath as his lips touched hers, lightly at first, then with more pressure. She slid her hands to his shoulders and moved the fingers of her right hand up to touch his stubbly cheek. Several moments later, Richard pulled back and inhaled a deep, shuddering breath. Charlotte pressed her lips together, savoring the kiss.

"I. . .uh. . ." Richard was the first to attempt to speak.

"Mr. Baxton?"

Charlotte and Richard stepped apart and turned to face a courier who held a message. Would there be no end to the interruptions this afternoon? And if a courier came all the way to the hospital to find Richard, it must be important. Charlotte silently prayed it wasn't bad news.

"Yes?" Richard replied.

"I have a message from the lawyer who serves your father's business, sir." The man handed over the note.

From a lawyer? This *was* serious.

Richard unfolded the single piece of paper and read it. Concern immediately creased his brow. A moment later, he reached into his vest pocket and handed a coin to the courier. "Thank you," he said. The courier left without a word.

Charlotte waited. What had the note said? And why did Richard appear so distraught?

Richard withdrew his pocket watch and flipped it open, then snapped it shut in haste and shoved it into his pocket. "Charlotte, I am sorry." He turned to face her, remorse reflecting in his eyes. "But I must leave on a trip to take care of an urgent family business matter. There is a train scheduled to depart immediately, and I must be on it. I do not know how long I will be gone, but I must see to this straightaway."

Charlotte nodded, even though she wanted to protest. "I understand. And I hope the matter is resolved quickly."

The ghost of a smile appeared on his face. "As do I. There is still so much here that needs to be done."

Did he mean in regard to Grace and her recovery or something pertaining to their relationship? He didn't elaborate. Instead, he took her hands in his.

"I do not wish to impose, but Mother should be here in about two hours. Until then, would you mind remaining here until Grace awakens from the anesthetic? I will be certain to leave instructions stating you are permitted to be with Grace. It isn't the ideal situation, but when she realizes I am not here, she will want to see a familiar face."

"Of course." How could she not stay? "I would be happy to see to it that Grace is both reassured and notified of your departure. You have no worries here."

"Thank you." Raising both her hands to his lips, he placed a kiss on each. "I promise to contact you as soon as I return."

With that, he was gone.

Charlotte watched as Richard stopped a nurse in the hall and spoke to her for a moment or two. The woman glanced at Charlotte then returned her attention to Richard, nodded, and appeared to reassure him. After responding to her, he gave Charlotte a final wave and disappeared through the double doors. The nurse went back to her work, and Charlotte stood in the alcove. What should she do now? The doctor or another staff member would get her once Grace awakened, or at least when they felt it was safe to move her to a bed in the children's ward where she'd reside until she was deemed healed enough to make the arduous journey home. Charlotte wanted to sit by the girl's bedside and hold her hand. At least that would give her something to occupy her time and mind.

The ending of this day had not gone how she planned.

Of course the kiss wasn't in her plan either. But she hadn't minded that at all. Now she had two things she needed to discuss with Richard. But he was gone, and she had no idea when he'd return. Left with no alternative, Charlotte again sat down on the bench. If she remembered correctly from her father's surgery a few years back, it shouldn't be long before the chloroform wore off and an attendant came to get her.

At least she had a few moments to herself to relax...*if* she could avoid dwelling on the memory of Richard's lips and the warmth of his embrace. That wouldn't be easy. She reached up and touched her fingers to her mouth, still feeling the tingle of his touch. His kiss had changed many things. Charlotte only prayed the change would be for the better.

twelve

Charlotte stood in the front hall as their butler closed the door behind her. Thomas Frederick Lyndhurst had just escorted her home after their sixth outing together in three weeks. As had been true of all their other outings, he'd been charming, engaging, and humorous. Charlotte managed a smile. Thomas certainly had his appealing characteristics. And his compelling cerulean eyes only enhanced his otherwise handsome features. But try as she might, she couldn't get Richard out of her thoughts.

She missed Grace as well. It had been three days since she'd penned a letter to the young girl, inquiring after her health and recovery status. A reply should be forthcoming any day.

"Oh good. You *have* returned." Bethany stood in the doorway of the parlor, stitching in hand. "Come, join Anastasia and me in here. We wish to hear all the details."

Sharing about her latest day out with Thomas didn't exactly occupy the top spot on Charlotte's list of things she would like to do, but talking with her sisters might help put her mind at ease. When she entered the room behind Bethany, she perched on the arm of the settee closest to the door. Picking up her needlework didn't appeal to her in the least, and she had no desire to remain in the parlor any longer than necessary.

"All right, tell us everything. And do not attempt to leave out any details." Anastasia pointed her long needle in Charlotte's direction, trying to appear stern but failing miserably.

Yes, Charlotte definitely needed this.

"Very well." She sighed. "I know you two will not give me a moment's rest until I appease your curiosity, so I may as well surrender now."

"Good." Bethany spoke up from her seat opposite Charlotte. "It would be futile to resist anyway. Anastasia and I always get what we want."

"Yes, I know." Charlotte pursed her lips. "And I am reminded of that nearly every time I hear Mother speak of her daughters."

Bethany waved off her defense. "Oh, that is only because Mother is more focused on seeing you happily married with a secure future. Once you are, her efforts will turn to me." She cast a glance at her other sister. "Then Anastasia will be the favorite."

"What do you mean 'will be'?" Anastasia narrowed her eyes at Bethany. "I already am. And as I am the youngest, I likely always will."

Bethany dropped her stitching to her lap and held up her hands in mock surrender. "All right. All right. You win. You are Mother and Father's favorite. And no one can take that away from you." She gave Anastasia a pointed glance. "Now, shall we return to the reason for this conversation?"

"There truly isn't much to tell," Charlotte replied. "It was a day much like the others I've spent with him. We took a walk along the creek, and he asked me how the bookshop was faring. Then he explained some about his work in textile manufacturing. He made a point to tell me he was poised to assume control in less than three years."

"And he will likely want to have his family already established before that occurs." Bethany raised one eyebrow in her sister's direction. "A point, I am certain, not lost on either Mr. Lyndhurst or Mother and Father."

Bethany had that right. From the moment Mother and Father mentioned Thomas to her a month ago, she knew how pleased they would be to see a successful match made. And as promised, she had been giving him a fair chance. But that might not be enough.

"Yes," Charlotte replied. "While Mr. Lyndhurst has not been so forward as to intimate that point, it is clear in the selected topics of conversation and in his mannerisms that he sees our time together as pursuing a purpose." She looked up at the floral pattern of the wallpaper opposite her. It reminded her of the room where Grace had received her presents at her birthday party. "However, try as I might," she continued, bringing her focus back to the subject at hand, "I am not certain I am being fair to him."

Anastasia nodded. "And you cannot help but make comparisons between Mr. Lyndhurst and Mr. Baxton. Correct?"

Charlotte sighed. Why did she even attempt to hide it? Yes, her sisters knew her better than anyone. But even the average passerby would be able to observe her behavior when in Thomas's company and see her heart wasn't in it. Maybe she just needed more time. Or perhaps she needed to allow her heart and mind to be open to the possibilities.

"Have you received any word at all since his departure?" Bethany asked, her face reflecting compassion and understanding.

"Not even a quickly scrawled note letting me know everything is all right." Charlotte glanced down at her hands.

"And what about Grace?" Anastasia asked. "Have you heard anything from her or seen her since the operation?"

"Yes. We have written, and I have paid her one brief visit thus far. I did write to her again just a few days ago. I expect I'll receive a reply very soon."

At least, Charlotte hoped Grace would again reply. She didn't see any reason why the girl wouldn't. Grace had responded promptly to the other two missives Charlotte sent. Unlike Richard. Just thinking about the situation sent her into a melancholic state. Why couldn't she have things back the way they were just before Grace's operation? Life had been so simple, so unencumbered. Then there was the operation, the special kiss she shared with Richard, and him being called away on urgent business. Charlotte didn't know what to do anymore.

"That's it," Anastasia spoke out. "I simply cannot sit here and abide this any longer."

Bethany and Charlotte both stared at their younger sister.

"Abide what?" Bethany asked.

Anastasia aimlessly waved her hand in Charlotte's direction, gesturing up and down. "This. . .this downhearted and dismal state our sister is in." She stowed her needlepoint material and supplies in the basket next to her then hopped to her feet, making a beeline for Charlotte. "Come on," she said without preamble, grabbing Charlotte's hand and pulling her toward the door. "We are leaving." She glanced over her shoulder. "Are you coming, Bethany?"

Charlotte planted her feet and halted their progress. "Where are we going?"

Bethany stood, not appearing in any great hurry to join them. "Yes. Where *are* we going?"

Anastasia looked as if someone had delivered a personal insult to her. "I cannot believe you two are not following my thought process." She held up Charlotte's hand and pointed at it. "Our dear sister here is in dire need of something to take her mind off her current worrisome problems. There is no better place than down at the beaver pond." She smiled in triumph, like a barn cat proud to bring his latest catch. "The antics of the beaver pups always put us in a more jovial frame of mind. I *would* suggest a visit to the marketplace and a tour through the dress shops." She cast a sly smile at Charlotte. "But that will never do. Nature has always been your area of interest."

Charlotte glanced at Bethany, who shrugged. Their sister was right. What could it hurt to have a change of scenery and do something different for a change? At the very least, it would be an enjoyable afternoon with her sisters, and they'd be back in time for dinner.

"Well?" Anastasia tapped her slippered foot. "Are we going or not?"

&

Dear Miss Pringle,

I received your note yesterday and did not want to wait another moment to reply. Recovery continues to go well, and I am increasing my movement every day. The doctor says I am his best patient, but I think he only says that so I will try harder. I have not heard much from Uncle Richard, but he sent word to say he misses me and had to go to New York. I guess that means he will be gone a little longer still. I miss him and pray he is not too lonely wherever he is. It would make me very happy if you could come see me again. Please come soon. It is hard being here with only Grandmother, the house staff, and the nurse who is taking care of me. I look forward to you coming.

Yours sincerely,
Grace

Charlotte pressed the folded note to her chest, closed her eyes, and took a deep breath. Grace wanted to see her again! And she wanted it to be as soon as possible.

"Is that a letter from Grace?" Anastasia approached from the side hallway, licking her fingers free of what appeared to be chocolate icing. "What does she say?"

"She's doing quite well in her recovery, but she's lonely." Charlotte tapped the note against her lips.

"So, why don't we go see her? I would welcome the excuse for a little journey away from the house. Summer sometimes is the most difficult season."

Charlotte stared at her sister. Could they do it? Would Mother and Father allow them to go? The first visit had been to check on Grace right after the surgery. This would be a purely social visit to the home of the very man against which her parents had cautioned her.

"Perhaps you should ask Mother and Father," Charlotte suggested to her sister. "You will likely have far greater success than if I mentioned it."

Anastasia shrugged. "Very well. I do not mind." She bounded off in search of their parents.

A little over an hour later, the two sisters were ready to depart. Already eager to make the journey to Ashbourne Hills, Charlotte had the butler arrange for a carriage to be brought around front. No sense dawdling and keeping young Grace waiting.

They didn't have to worry about arriving at an inconvenient time. As soon as the Baxton's butler stood in the doorway to the drawing room and announced Charlotte and Anastasia's arrival, Grace squealed. Charlotte waited for the man to step around her before she and her sister entered to see Grace sitting upright on a sofa. A quick glance around the room revealed a makeshift cot that no doubt served as a bed, a pair of crutches propped against the sofa, and a rather substantial pile of books on the table near Grace.

"Miss Pringle! Anastasia! You came!" Grace placed both hands on either side of her legs and bounced up and down. As her note said, she seemed to be doing rather well. "I had hoped you would get my note and come straightaway. And you did."

Charlotte smiled. "Of course I did. You didn't think I could stay away any longer, now did you? And I brought Anastasia as an added bonus." She walked toward the sofa and dropped down to be at eye level with Grace. "Besides. You are not the only one who is missing someone these days."

Grace extended her arms, and Charlotte shifted to her knees to give the girl a hug. Oh, it was so good to be with her again and to see her in such a cheerful state. Despite her circumstances and what had to be a rather painful set of exercises set up as an aid to her full recovery, Grace remained positive and buoyant. Perhaps Charlotte should take lessons from the young girl.

After pulling back, Charlotte peered into Grace's face. "Your letter said the doctor considered you his best patient. I take it that means your recovery is going well?"

"Yes." Grace smiled. "Do you want to see what I can do already?"

The girl seemed so eager, but was it wise for her to exert herself so much? "I don't know, Grace. I do not wish you to harm yourself by attempting to do more than you're able at this point."

"Yes," Anastasia added, looking from the crutches to the wheeled chair to Grace and back again, appearing uncertain. "You should take it easy."

"I promise I will take it slow." She turned and looked over her shoulder. "Laura, could you come help me please?"

The nursemaid approached, looking more like a lady's maid than a trained nurse. But if she accomplished what Grace's doctor wanted, that was the important part. Laura handed Grace the crutches, and Charlotte backed out of the way. Laura then reached for Grace's arms to help bring her to her feet. At that point, Grace placed the crutches under her arms and slowly bore all her weight on her legs.

Charlotte watched with baited breath. Amazing. This girl had gone from being confined to a wheeled chair to standing in just five weeks. When Grace started to take a step, Charlotte inhaled sharply. "Grace, be careful!"

"It is quite all right, Miss Pringle," Laura replied with

a reassuring smile. "Grace has mastered this several times already."

The warning came out automatically. She should have known Laura wouldn't let Grace do anything the doctor hadn't instructed her to do. But Charlotte couldn't help it. The protective instinct seemed so natural. And in a way, she felt responsible for Grace. Richard might not have left her fully in charge, but his parting words had been to ask her to be there when Grace awoke. So in a small way, she served as his proxy in his absence. Not that Grace's grandmother couldn't perform that role. Charlotte merely felt she owed it to Grace.

With a deep breath to calm her nerves, Charlotte stepped back again and took a seat in the nearest chair. She bit her lip to keep from calling out any more words of caution. Laura had things well under control, and Grace didn't appear to be overexerting herself or to be in any kind of pain. Before she knew it, Grace changed directions and headed her way. In no time at all, she stood in front of Charlotte, grinning from ear to ear.

"I did it! I did it!" the girl cried. "I actually walked."

"Wow!" Anastasia stared, clearly impressed.

Charlotte cupped Grace's face between her hands and placed a kiss on the girl's forehead. "Yes you did. And you are looking quite well, too. I don't think your doctor jested when he called you his best patient. I believe you are. You should be proud of all you've accomplished."

"All right, Grace," Laura admonished. "It's time for you to rest. I shall be sure to make note of your progress so the doctor can adjust the next schedule of exercises if necessary."

Laura helped Grace back to the sofa and returned the crutches to their resting place. She poured a glass of water and handed it to Grace.

"Thank you very much, Laura," Grace replied. She took

a sip and swallowed. "Now, if you do not mind, could you leave Miss Pringle, her sister, and me to talk privately? I have something I wish to ask."

"Very well, Miss Grace." Laura made her way to the door, turning as she reached it. "I shall be just outside should you need me."

Charlotte raised her eyebrows as the door clicked shut behind the nursemaid. Grace had something she wanted to discuss? What could it be? The girl looked so serious.

"So," Grace began, folding her hands in her lap. "You said when you arrived I wasn't the only one who had been missing someone lately."

Had she really said that? Surely it was in reference to missing Grace. Wasn't it? She didn't know if she wanted to acknowledge anything else right now. But Grace wasn't about to let her get off so easily, not if that look in her eyes was any indication.

"Are you saying you have been missing someone other than me?"

The girl's piercing gaze seemed to see right through her. Charlotte shifted in her seat. Oh, how easy it would be to refute that question. But that meant Charlotte would have to lie.

"Of course she is," Anastasia burst out.

"I knew it!" Grace snapped her fingers and grinned. "You *do* miss Uncle Richard. I can see it in your eyes."

There was no point in denying it now. "Yes." Charlotte sighed. "I do." She brightened. "But I believe I missed you more."

Grace giggled. "I don't think so." Again, the intent gaze returned. "Do you love him?"

Charlotte's breath hitched. She tried to swallow past the lump in her throat. "Pardon me?" Her voice came out sounding more like a croak. She cleared her throat. "What did you ask?"

"I asked if you love Uncle Richard. He talks about you all the time, so I know he cares about you."

"I. . .uh. . .that is. . .I'm not certain I have an answer to that." Wonderful. A twelve-year-old girl asks her about her feelings, and she stumbles through a reply. She couldn't even come up with a viable answer. And the answer she *did* give was even more revealing. "It doesn't usually take a lot of thought. Either you love someone or you don't. That should be easy enough to know."

"Actually, Grace, it's not that simple." If only it were. "There is far more involved with loving someone than simply admitting it or knowing it. And right now, I do not know for certain."

"And he hasn't written to Charlotte." Anastasia jutted her chin in the air. "You would think if Charlotte was so special and if he cared about her, he would keep in touch."

"I am sure he would write if he could," Grace said in her uncle's defense. "But he is probably very busy and cannot find the time."

Ah, the innocence. Charlotte wished she could believe as Grace did or even trust for that matter. Things were left so unsettled between her and Richard, though. They didn't have time to discuss the kiss they shared or what that meant to their relationship. How could she begin to sort through the confusing haze of her feelings? But she needed to come up with some sort of answer for Grace.

Charlotte knelt in front of Grace again and took the girl's hands in hers. "Grace, I appreciate your reassurance. I *do* care for your uncle. You both are very special to me. But so many other factors are at play in this situation." Not the least of which was her relationship with Thomas Lyndhurst. Grace didn't need to know about that, but she did deserve an honest response to her statement about Richard's reasons for not writing. "And your uncle's notes home or lack thereof are only a small part of the situation. Please understand me when I say I wish there was a simple solution. For now, let us leave it at you both being a very important part of my life. Anything other than that, we shall have to wait and see."

Grace nodded. "I do understand, Miss Pringle. But I also am certain it will all work out. Have faith."

ॐ

Faith. Grace made it sound so simple. But another month had passed and still no word from Richard. Grace wrote to say he was now in Boston and would be home as soon as he could. The news didn't make Charlotte feel any better, though. And if he could write to Grace, why hadn't he taken an extra moment or two to write to her? True, he didn't owe her an explanation, and neither one of them had declared any intentions toward the other.

Still, it was hard not feeling neglected and forgotten in everything. Two months, and she didn't know any more now than she did when Richard left that day at the hospital. So each time Thomas came to call, she had no good reason to turn away his suit.

One evening in early September, they sat together on a bench in the park. Charlotte kept her hands folded in her lap as she looked out across the small acreage. The silence pounded against her ears. Why had Thomas been so quiet tonight? Normally by now he'd have delivered several jokes or shared a few tidbits on his daily work. But not tonight.

"Miss Pringle. . .uh. . .Charlotte," he said softly.

Charlotte leaned closer to hear better. "Yes, Mr. Lyndhurst. . . I mean. . .Thomas."

He avoided looking at her and stared straight ahead. "What I have to say tonight is not easy, but I ask that you hear me out fully before you say anything."

She nodded, wishing she could see his eyes. He turned her way, and she wished he hadn't. Resignation and pain danced with a certain dismal determination.

"I am no fool. I have known for quite some time that your heart is not fully engaged in our courtship."

Charlotte's shoulders fell. He stated it so plainly, without any rancor or condemnation. Yet she felt the sting of his words just as deeply.

"That does not change the fact that our families would like to see a union forged between us. And I must say, I cannot see any reason why that shouldn't occur. You possess a great deal of intelligence, and your ability to manage your bookshop will aid you in the managing of a household." He reached for her hands and held them loosely in his own, centering his focus on her in an unwavering gaze. "I know I am not saying this in the best manner possible, but I have grown quite fond of you in our time together the past two months. And I believe given more time, our relationship will become much dearer."

He reached into his vest pocket, and a moment later the moonlight glinted off the gemstones of a beautiful amethyst, sapphire, and emerald ring. Charlotte gasped. Could he really be doing this? Right here? Right now?

"Forgive me for not presenting this with more preamble. But I feel any further delays are unnecessary." He cleared his throat. "I would like to ask you to be my wife, with all the affection and honor I hold for you. Everything I have will be yours, and our alliance will secure the future for us both."

Well, it certainly wasn't the romantic proposal she'd envisioned. *Practical* seemed to be the best word Charlotte could find to describe it. But Thomas was sincere. And he was right. Further delays wouldn't change anything other than to delay the inevitable. She would be twenty-one next month. A spinster by anyone's determination. Her parents were eager to see her wed, and she needed to make a decision. As much as it pained her to admit it, she needed to face the facts. Richard didn't care for her as she thought he might. Otherwise, he would have found a way to notify her by now. Marriage to Thomas was a good match. She could certainly do much worse.

A resigned sigh escaped her lips as she regarded the ring Thomas held out in front of her. Charlotte really didn't have much choice. She mustered up her best attempt at a smile and extended her right hand toward him. "I should like a week to ponder this before I give you my answer. Until then, I trust you will not be offended if I ask you to keep this ring in your possession."

Thomas returned the ring to his vest pocket then leaned forward and placed a chaste kiss on her cheek. "I promise I will do everything in my power to make you happy. Please notify me as soon as you come to a decision. If your answer is a positive one, I'd like to announce this as soon as possible."

Charlotte didn't trust her voice. She nodded instead.

Thomas rose and drew her up with him. "Come, let us seek out your parents and tell them the good news. They are going to be quite pleased, I am sure."

Yes, they would. But Charlotte was certain it would be some time before she would share in that pleasure.

❧

Richard ran his hands through his hair. He didn't care if the ends stood out. All he wanted was a conclusion to this entire ordeal. It had stretched on long enough. And he didn't appreciate being dragged to New York as well as Boston in order to settle his brother's affairs pertaining to their shipping business. Richard had always been in charge of the building part of the company. Elliott was the businessman. But now Richard was left to clean up the mess.

Two entire months. It should have been settled in one week or less. When he left, he thought that was all it would take. Then he could return to Charlotte and pick up where they'd left off. Now, he wasn't so sure. He'd been gone a long time. He'd written, but she had yet to reply in any way. And he'd been sure to leave a valid address where he could be reached should a response be sent. He had walked out on her after sharing a kiss. Although his notes had expressed how much he'd missed her and looked forward to seeing her again, the words felt superficial. But oh, the memory of her upturned face and the soft feel of her lips. It was enough to distract a man for days. And he'd had two months to dwell on it. Months that allowed him to realize what he needed to do.

As he stepped on the train at the New York and New England terminal in Boston, Richard prayed the ride would pass quickly. Where Charlotte was concerned, he also prayed he wasn't too late.

thirteen

No! No, it couldn't be. Richard closed his eyes and opened them again, as if doing so would erase the dreadful tidings that greeted him in black and white upon his arrival home. But the *Gazette* didn't lie. He had been reading the paper in the carriage and only just reached the society section. What he read caused his heart to drop. Charlotte had been seen repeatedly on the arm of a Mr. Thomas Frederick Lyndhurst, and rumors had it an engagement might be forthcoming.

He was too late.

Richard silently cursed the timing of his trip. Had he been home when he thought, he could have straightened everything out, and Charlotte wouldn't be seeing this other man now. He was certain of it. Now what was he going to do?

"Uncle Richard! You're back!" Grace called out across the front hall.

Richard turned to see his niece using only a single crutch for support. "Grace! You're walking!" Knowing of her progress from the letters he'd received during his absence paled in comparison to seeing the reality right before his eyes. He really *had* been gone too long. He'd missed so much, and he'd never get that time back. After laying the evening edition on the hall table, he opened his arms wide and waited for Grace to jump into them. Oh, it felt so good to have his niece back.

Grace kissed his cheek then looked over his shoulder. "I see you have read the newspaper."

Richard angled his head back and sighed. "Yes. And it came as quite a surprise, I must say."

"I only heard about it two days ago, and I still can't believe it."

"Well, it's right there." He lowered his niece to the floor. "Her family has allowed the information to be printed in the society column, so it must be true."

Grace took up her crutch again and leaned on it. "But how could she do this to you? She loves you."

Obviously not or she wouldn't have rushed off to be courted by another man. He wasn't about to share that spiteful remark with his niece, though. "Miss Pringle must have decided otherwise, Grace," he said instead. "There is nothing I can do about it now."

"Yes there is," Grace protested. "You can go find her and tell her you love her, too. Then she can cease spending time with this other gentleman and the two of you can get married, the way it's supposed to be."

If only he *could* do that. Richard slipped off his coat and hat and allowed the butler to take his things. "I'm sorry, but it's too late. I cannot and will not interfere in her happiness or the choice she's made."

"It's not too late." Grace stamped her foot. "And she can't possibly be happy if she isn't with you." She grabbed hold of his arm and compelled him to look down at her. "I know she isn't, Uncle Richard. She told me so."

Richard widened his eyes. "What?"

"Miss Pringle came to visit me while you were away, and I asked her if she loved you."

"Grace," he scolded. "It wasn't your place to ask her something like that. I am rather displeased to hear you did so." Although he wanted to hear Charlotte's answer.

Grace dipped her chin. "I am sorry, Uncle Richard, but she spoke of missing both of us and said she had come to care for us a great deal."

That was a start. But it wasn't exactly what he wanted to hear. Richard drew his niece to one of two chairs next to each other. Once they were both seated, he replied. "Caring for someone is not the same as loving them."

"I know." She nodded. "But Miss Pringle said a lot of other factors were involved and that we both were very special to her." Grace pressed her lips into a thin line and gave him a rather determined stare. "I am telling you, Uncle Richard. She loves you. And it's not too late if she's not yet engaged. You still have time. But not if you don't believe."

His niece was nothing if not adamant when she set her mind on something. "Believe what?" he asked, drawing his eyebrows together.

"Believe God knows best, and He is watching over both of you," she replied. "Believe He wants you both to be happy and that won't happen if you're not together. And believe He brought you home at just the right time to do something about it."

Richard shook his head. He had to admit, Grace made a valid point. Were she a young lad, he might envision her growing up to become a lawyer one day. For now, though, she turned her argumentative prowess on him. And he wasn't sure he could come up with a valid rebuttal.

A chuckle escaped his lips, and he held up his hands. "All right. All right. You win," he said with a smile. After tousling her hair, he stood and called for the butler. "I cannot guarantee the outcome will be as you or I hope, but I will promise to try."

"You can do it, Uncle Richard," Grace said with triumphant certainty. "I know it will all work out."

&

Richard paused just outside the door to Mr. Pringle's study. The butler had directed him down the hall and said Mr. Pringle was expecting him. Of course he was. Richard had penned a formal missive and requested this meeting almost immediately after arriving home and reading that dreadful news in the *Gazette*. Now that he was here, his stomach clenched and tension rippled across his shoulders.

With a quick prayer for strength, he took a deep breath and raised his hand to deliver two short knocks to the closed door.

"Come in!" came the immediate response.

He turned the knob and pushed the door open, stepping into the darkened interior and immediately removing his hat. His eyes searched the room and found Mr. Pringle standing next to his desk. The man's expression was too difficult to read from this distance, though.

"Mr. Pringle," Richard plunged forward. "Thank you for seeing me on such short notice."

"It is my pleasure, Mr. Baxton."

Charlotte's father didn't make any attempt to move from where he stood, so Richard approached him instead.

"I know you probably have a lot of business to attend to, so I won't take up too much of your time. I wanted to come here today to speak to you in person about your daughter Charlotte."

"When I received your note, I had a distinct feeling what this meeting would be about." The man brushed his fingers across his clean-shaven chin. "Quite frankly, I am surprised it has taken you so long to see me again."

"Yes. I was called away unexpectedly on business that kept me away longer than I thought it might. I had to make two additional journeys to New York and Boston and only arrived home yesterday."

"And what exactly was that business?"

Richard tilted his head. "As you know from our earlier conversation, sir, my family has been involved in the ship-building business for three generations. We have financial holdings in almost all of the major ports along the Atlantic Coast. The trouble began when my brother was killed in a carriage accident many months back."

"I was sorry to hear of your loss, son." His voice showed his sincerity.

"Thank you." Richard took a breath. "In short, I was left everything, but there was a seize on the profits and a delay in the ownership transfer. While our lawyer sorted through the mounds of paperwork and legal barriers, I was here caring for my niece and doing what I could to keep everything running. This recent journey finally resolved all the issues and the full transfer is now complete."

"I am sure that brings you a sense of relief."

"Yes, it does. But that pales in comparison to the surprise that awaited me in the evening edition of the *Wilmington Gazette* upon my return. I didn't wish to waste any more time than I had already lost, so I requested this meeting straightaway."

"I'm glad you did come, son, in spite of the current circumstances. It says much about you and your level of devotion to my daughter."

Richard licked his lips and shifted from one foot to the other, turning his hat in his hands. Mr. Pringle's approval meant so much. He'd dealt with industry and manufacturing magnates without missing a breath, but standing before this man put him on edge.

"I won't deny that I've been aware of Charlotte's feelings for you for quite some time now, even when she attempted to say otherwise. And I won't make you any more uncomfortable than you are by asking your intentions toward my daughter. I am certain they are honorable."

"Yes sir."

Mr. Pringle nodded. "Very well. Then, the only other issue at hand is the present status of my daughter's affections. As you are aware, she has been courted by Mr. Lyndhurst of Greenville these recent weeks." He held up a hand, palm outward. "I might have given my consent to the union, but the ultimate decision lies with Charlotte." The hint of a grin tugged at the corners of the man's mouth. "And if I know my daughter, I have a feeling a more personal conversation with her will be forthcoming rather soon."

Richard swallowed and nodded, unable to speak beyond the tightness in his throat. Did this mean the man was giving his consent for Richard to call on Charlotte as well and offer his proposal?

"You will find my daughter at the bookshop, son."

Obviously, he was.

"And if you do not wish to miss your chance, I would suggest you depart here immediately."

Richard straightened. "Oh! Yes. I will."

"Good. We will leave the rest of the details for a later time. Now if you'll excuse me, I do have some rather important matters that require my attention before dinner." He winked. "And I don't wish to upset Mrs. Pringle by being late."

"No, sir!" Richard grinned, grateful he'd again found his voice.

"I trust you don't mind seeing yourself out?"

"Not at all, sir." Richard turned toward the door then glanced over his shoulder. "Thank you again, Mr. Pringle."

"You're quite welcome."

⁂

Richard peered in through the windows. The bookshop looked empty. He didn't see Charlotte anywhere. Perfect. She wouldn't see him come in. But she *would* hear him. Slowly, he opened the door, praying he wouldn't trigger the bell. So far, so good. He made it inside without announcing his presence. Now he had to find Charlotte.

That didn't take long. She stood on a stool at the far end of the first aisle, reaching to the top shelf but falling just short. Richard moved in silence and came up behind her, retrieving the book she sought and putting it in her hand.

She didn't even turn around. "Thank you."

"You're welcome." His voice cracked, and the two words came out in a combination cough and squeak. Richard cleared his throat, and tried again. "You're welcome."

Charlotte spun around. "Richard!"

She almost lost her balance, but he put his hands to her waist to steady her. As soon as she righted herself, he dropped his hands to his sides. Of course, he wanted to keep them there. Wanted to lift her down from the stool and into his arms. But he didn't have that right. She was almost engaged to another. And until that situation was rectified, he had to keep his distance. Or at least try.

"I'm surprised to see you here." Her voice had a hardened edge to it, and her eyes held a mixture of remorse and regret. "Did you not have other business to attend to?"

Ouch. But he deserved that. He had all but abandoned her, and now, two months later, he expected a warm welcome? What had he been thinking? He had written but never received a reply, so there was no guarantee his letters had even been received. He intended to find out.

Richard looked up at her. "Could you please come down off the stool? I would much rather speak with you on a more even level."

She did as he asked, but her entire demeanor remained cool, reserved. If she *had* received his letters, would she still be acting this way?

"Charlotte, I know my appearance here is unexpected and possibly unwanted. I probably shouldn't have come at all." Despite having told himself many times that he'd done what he had to do, Richard couldn't keep the self-condemnation from his voice.

Charlotte closed her eyes. The soft sounds of her breathing accompanied the faint *clip-clop* of horses' hooves and carriage wheels on the cobblestones outside. When her eyelids opened again, the same doubt, uncertainty, and fear he felt reflected back at him.

"Richard, we shouldn't be—"

"Shh." He cut her off and touched two fingers to her lips then removed his hand. She stared at him with doe-like innocence. "Let me go first."

An almost imperceptible nod followed his entreaty. All right. He had her undivided attention. Now what should he say?

"Charlotte, I repeated in my mind what I would say to you during the ride over here. And I owe you an apology." There, that wasn't such a bad start. "I left you standing in the hospital with a promise to contact you as soon as I returned home. But a trip I believed would take me just a week ended up taking me two months. In all that time, although I sent a handful of letters to let you know what was happening, I never received a response. Still, the letters did not come close to conveying how I truly felt, and you deserved more than that." He implored her with his gaze. "Can you forgive me?"

It hadn't come out the way he'd rehearsed it in his head, but it could still work. He hoped it would.

"You wrote to me?" Surprise and tender awe blended on her face as her eyes shimmered with unshed tears. "I never received a single note."

Well, that explained a lot. "I feared that might be the case," he said instead. "Nevertheless, I stand before you now, asking your forgiveness."

Charlotte took several moments before responding. "Of course I forgive you."

It wasn't much, but it was a start. "Thank you." Richard clenched his fists at his side, wanting more than anything to take Charlotte's hands in his. But not yet. "I know my timing is rather flawed and imperfect. But I came at the first opportunity. And while I do not hold any misconceptions that you will respond the way I would like, I could not in good conscience leave things unresolved between us." He had to get this out now, or he might lose his nerve. "There. . . there's one more thing."

Her eyes seemed to tell him to go on, but the words died in his throat. Perhaps making her smile would lighten the mood a bit and help him say what he came to tell her. It might not work, but he had to try *something*.

"At least I know I have a captive audience."

That worked. A slow smile tugged at her lips, even though it didn't quite meet her eyes. Yes. That's just what he needed to help him get through the next part of his confession. He braved reaching for her hands to clasp them between both of his. She didn't pull away.

"Charlotte, it took a longer-than-expected journey to make me realize just how special you are to me. I'm a fool for not seeing it sooner. That kiss we shared at the hospital shook me right to the core. I didn't know how to respond. I could dare to hope only that you felt the same as I." He sought her gaze and held it. "Maybe I didn't want to believe it. Maybe I wasn't ready. I don't know. What I do know is I don't want to lose you."

A sharp gasp followed his declaration. This was it. He had to say it now.

"Charlotte, I love you. I've probably loved you for a while now. I was just too blind to see it. And I know you are being courted by another, with rumors stating an engagement is forthcoming. But I have your father's permission to ask you—if you can find any fondness at all for me in your heart, please. I beg of you. Do not continue to accept Mr. Lyndhurst's suit."

Charlotte's hands moved beneath his, and she turned her wrist to interlace their fingers. He glanced down at their joined hands then back at her face. Tenderness replaced the uncertainty of a moment before. Her lips moved, but no sound came out. Then she seemed to find her voice.

"Before I say anything else, I want to say I was deeply hurt by your silence and the increasing time you were away. I thought I did something wrong. That I somehow caused your silence. That you were possibly ashamed for having kissed me and didn't know how to take it back. Then my parents pushed me toward Mr. Lyndhurst, and as your absence lengthened, I felt I was left with no choice." She averted her eyes. "So I agreed to allow him to court me. But I was wrong for doubting you and for believing you had intentionally abandoned me. Can *you* forgive *me*?"

He didn't hesitate. "Yes. Of course I will." How could he deny her what she'd just given him only a few moments ago?

She visibly relaxed. After a shuddering breath, she again met his gaze with tears glistening in her eyes. "Richard, I love you, too."

He grinned and slid to one knee on the floor, right there in the dusty aisle of the bookshop. But he didn't care. He reached into his coat and pulled out his grandmother's ring. A diamond-accented sapphire with lighter blue topaz around the rim. He held it up to Charlotte, all the love he felt inside ready to burst. "Then will you marry me?"

A lone tear spilled and traced a wet path down her cheek. Richard reached up with his other hand and brushed it away. Silence descended, and the seconds ticked by in slow progression.

"I say," an unfamiliar but proper voice sounded from the front of the store. "It appears I have arrived in the middle of the most unfortunate circumstances." The gentleman paused. "At least for me."

Richard turned to look up the aisle and met the regretful gaze of a well-dressed gentleman about his age, only this man held an ornate cane in one hand and a top-quality top hat in the other. From the way Charlotte stiffened, this man could be only one person. Richard stood and raised his eyebrows. "Mr. Lyndhurst, I presume?"

"The very same," the man said with a succinct nod. He switched his cane to his left hand and extended his right. "And you must be Richard Baxton."

"Yes," Richard replied, returning the handshake.

"Well, I believe I have timed my appearance a mite too late." Lyndhurst gestured toward Charlotte and Richard and the close proximity in which the two stood. "Or perhaps I am right on time."

Charlotte started to turn toward Mr. Lyndhurst. "Thomas, I—"

But the man raised his hand that held the cane and lifted two fingers, effectively silencing whatever she'd been about to say. "Please, my dear Charlotte. You owe me no explanation." He softened his expression. "Only a fool would see the way you are looking at Mr. Baxton and not know of your fervent affection. It is not my place to interfere, nor would I consider it." Lyndhurst took two steps back and dipped his head, swinging wide the hand that held his top hat. "Now, if you will excuse me, I shall formally retract my suit and take my leave. I wish you both the utmost happiness."

Silence followed in the wake of Thomas's exit. Richard and Charlotte both stared up the aisle, as if the man hadn't really been there. Several moments later, Richard shook his head and turned again to face Charlotte. Resuming his position on bended knee, he again took her hands in his.

"I believe there is still a question waiting for an answer," he reminded her with a smile.

Charlotte startled and stared down at him. A dazed look clouded her eyes. Her mouth moved, but no words came out. It was as if she stood transfixed, held captive by the exchange that had just occurred.

"Say you will!" Grace's voice broke the spell.

Charlotte laughed, and Richard joined her. Just when had his niece snuck into the shop? And how had she done so without either of them hearing her? Then again, he had done it.

"It appears we have a curious little songbird in our midst," Charlotte said. "Bent on trilling out her own cadenza."

"Yes, she insisted upon accompanying me here. But this is a duet. At least for the moment." He cast a reproachful glance at his niece. "I instructed her to remain outside." He returned his gaze to Charlotte. "Even so, you know how Grace feels. I, on the other hand, remain down here awaiting *your* answer."

Lyrical laughter again escaped her lips. "Yes! Yes, of course I will marry you."

Richard nearly jumped to his feet and gave her a quick peck on the mouth. He pulled back to look down into her face, seeing the same longing he felt. He placed the symbol of their promise on her ring finger. Lowering his lips again, he positioned himself for a better, deeper kiss this time.

A few moments later, he pulled back and glanced to his left. A chuckle rumbled in his chest. He shared a special look with Charlotte, emboldened by her nod and the look of love in her eyes.

"Grace, you have already heard and seen everything. And we both know what you think. Now, will you perhaps leave us alone to discuss a few more things?"

Grace obviously took that as a sign to come closer. "There will be time enough for that later. Right now I want to celebrate with you both." She wrapped one arm around each of them.

Richard pivoted to face Charlotte. Amusement danced in her eyes. He shrugged. They still had so much to discuss. And Charlotte had yet to let her parents know of her decisions.

They could and would discuss the details of their engagement and wedding another time. Right now, Grace watched and smiled as though their entire relationship—friends to lovers—had been entirely of her making. Richard smiled. It had been by God's design all along.

epilogue

Charlotte leaned into Richard's casual yet affectionate embrace as she looked around at the friends and family gathered in her home. So much love and support. She could barely talk beyond the tightness in her throat. But talk, she must. Clearing her throat, she scanned the assemblage, searching for a certain twelve-year-old girl.

"Grace," she called out after locating her. "Would you please come join your uncle and me up front? I have something very special to present to you."

As Grace stepped out from the small crowd, Charlotte reached behind her for the carefully wrapped gift she'd prepared specifically for this day. The young girl—no, young *lady*—stood before Charlotte with an expectant smile on her face. Charlotte trailed her fingers down Grace's cheek and brushed back a few loose tendrils of hair.

"Grace, you already know how much your uncle and I love you. And we both look forward to welcoming you into our newly joined life together as soon as our wedding concludes. But for now, I would like you to have this."

She handed the gift to Grace, who took it and stared.

Charlotte nodded. "You may open it now."

Needing no further encouragement, Grace tore back the paper and withdrew the treasured book Charlotte had spent months attempting to find.

Grace looked down and read the title. "*Robinson Crusoe?*"

"Yes." Charlotte smoothed her hand over the cover. "This book once belonged to my great-grandmother's great-grandmother. It is a first edition with her dedication written

inside. I acquired it just prior to meeting you and your uncle."
She tilted her head to gaze up at Richard. He squeezed her
waist and smiled, love shining in his eyes. Returning her
attention to Grace, Charlotte smiled. "Now I would like you
to have it. It will be a constant reminder of how God used
books to bring us together and eventually make us a family."

Grace stared at the book, holding it in her hands like
fine porcelain. A moment later, she looked up at Charlotte,
then her uncle, then back to the book, and finally again at
Charlotte. "You are giving this to me? To keep?"

"Yes," Charlotte replied. "Because, I believe we share something very, very special." She winked. "An insatiable appetite for
good books. I spent a great deal of time locating this title, and
now you can have it for your own." She tipped up the girl's chin
with her forefinger. "But I have one requirement."

"What is that?"

"I only ask that you treasure it as much as I have, and when
the time comes for you to start a family of your own, you
keep this book as a gift for your daughter or son."

Grace pressed her lips tight, glancing again at the book.
"But don't you wish to keep this for your own children?"

Charlotte's throat clenched at the forlorn quality in
Grace's voice. Richard squeezed her waist again then reached
out and brushed Grace's cheek. Charlotte did the same. But
Richard spoke.

"You are every bit as much our daughter as any children we
might have in the future. So this book belongs to you, and we
know you will take excellent care of it."

Grace smiled, the sheen of tears magnifying the joy in her
eyes. "Oh yes!" she said, and hugged the book to her chest.
"I shall be certain to care for and keep this book in the best
condition possible. And I shall treasure it always."

"Now," Richard shifted, removing his arm from around
Charlotte's waist to bend to eye level with his niece. "What

do you say we resume the engagement party and get things under way?"

Grace brightened then turned to face everyone else. With one hand sweeping out across the crowd, she announced, "Let the celebration commence!"

Rumbles of laughter and exclamations of delight sounded forth from family and friends. Grace skipped away, and Richard returned to Charlotte.

With a roguish grin, he winked and touched his forehead to hers. "We are going to have our hands full for the next few years."

Charlotte smiled, her face warming rapidly, as she reached to place a chaste kiss on his lips. "I wouldn't have it any other way."

A Letter To Our Readers

Dear Reader:

In order that we might better contribute to your reading enjoyment, we would appreciate your taking a few minutes to respond to the following questions. We welcome your comments and read each form and letter we receive. When completed, please return to the following:

Fiction Editor
Heartsong Presents
PO Box 719
Uhrichsville, Ohio 44683

1. Did you enjoy reading *Bound by Grace* by Amber Stockton?
   ❏ Very much! I would like to see more books by this author!
   ❏ Moderately. I would have enjoyed it more if

   _____

   _____

   _____

2. Are you a member of **Heartsong Presents**? ❏ Yes ❏ No
   If no, where did you purchase this book? _____

   _____

3. How would you rate, on a scale from 1 (poor) to 5 (superior), the cover design? _____

4. On a scale from 1 (poor) to 10 (superior), please rate the following elements.

   ____ Heroine   ____ Plot
   ____ Hero   ____ Inspirational theme
   ____ Setting   ____ Secondary characters

5. These characters were special because? _____

_____

_____

6. How has this book inspired your life? _____

_____

_____

7. What settings would you like to see covered in future **Heartsong Presents** books? _____

_____

_____

8. What are some inspirational themes you would like to see treated in future books? _____

_____

_____

9. Would you be interested in reading other **Heartsong Presents** titles? ❏ Yes ❏ No

10. Please check your age range:

❏ Under 18   ❏ 18-24
❏ 25-34   ❏ 35-45
❏ 46-55   ❏ Over 55

Name _____

Occupation _____

Address _____

City, State, Zip _____

E-mail _____